Hi, I'm JIMMY!

Like me, you probably noticed the world is run by adults.

But ask yourself: Who would do the best job
of making books that *kids* will love?

Yeah. **Kids!**

So that's how the idea of JIMMY books came to life.

We want every JIMMY book to be so good that when you're finished,
you'll say,

"PLEASE GIVE ME ANOTHER BOOK!"

Give this one a try and see if you agree.

(If not, you're probably an adult!)

JAMES PATTERSON

PRAISE FOR **MIDDLE SCHOOL**

"A perfectly pitched novel."
> —*Los Angeles Times*

"Rafe is a bad boy with a heart of gold."
> —*The New York Times*

"Sure to appeal!"
> —*Booklist*

"Rafe [is] a realistic kid whom readers would want as a friend and coconspirator."
> —*School Library Journal*

"Will be enjoyed by middle-grade boys, particularly reluctant readers."
> —*VOYA*

"Will keep [readers] laughing and engaged."
> —*Children's Literature*

PRAISE FOR **HOUSE OF ROBOTS**

"Underlying the novel's laughs are themes of friendship, compassion, and family....Neufeld's raucous cartoons and comics sequences amp up the comedy with slapstick action, metafictional gags, and lots of robo-gadgetry."
> —*Publishers Weekly*

"Plenty of amusing jokes...Young readers with an interest in science will certainly be engaged."
> —*Kirkus Reviews*

"A good fit for reluctant readers."
> —*Common Sense Media*

GETS KIDS READING!

MIDDLE SCHOOL
SCHOOL

ULTIMATE SHOWDOWN

JAMES PATTERSON

AND JULIA BERGEN

ILLUSTRATED BY
ALEC LONGSTRETH

JIMMY PATTERSON BOOKS
LITTLE, BROWN AND COMPANY
NEW YORK · BOSTON · LONDON

This book would not have been possible
without the help of Frank Nicolo, Ned Rust,
Lindsay Cliett, Gregg Wasiak, and Chris Grabenstein.
Many thanks for all your hard work
in making this book come together.
—J.P.

Copyright © 2014 by James Patterson
Illustrations by Alec Longstreth
Excerpt from *Treasure Hunters* copyright © 2013 by James Patterson
Illustrations by Juliana Neufeld

JIMMY Patterson Books / Little, Brown and Company
Hachette Book Group
1290 Avenue of the Americas, New York, NY 10104
jimmypatterson.org

First Edition: March 2014

JIMMY Patterson Books is an imprint of Little, Brown and Company, a division of Hachette Book Group, Inc. The Little, Brown name and logo are trademarks of Hachette Book Group, Inc. The JIMMY Patterson name and logo are trademarks of JBP Business, LLC.

The publisher is not responsible for websites (or their content) that are not owned by the publisher.

The Hachette Speakers Bureau provides a wide range of authors for speaking events. To find out more, go to hachettespeakersbureau.com or call (866) 376-6591.

Library of Congress Cataloging-in-Publication Data

Patterson, James, 1947– author.

Ultimate showdown / James Patterson and Julia Bergen ;
illustrated by Alec Longstreth. — First edition.

pages cm. — (Middle school)

Summary: Opinionated siblings Rafe and Georgia Khatchadorian debate a variety of topics relating to the ups and downs of middle school life and encourage readers to add their own contributions through write-in games and activities.

ISBN 978-0-316-32211-9 (paper over board) — ISBN 978-0-316-32378-9 (international)
[1. Middle schools—Fiction. 2. Schools—Fiction. 3. Brothers and sisters—Fiction.
4. Humorous stories.] I. Bergen, Julia, author. II. Longstreth, Alec, illustrator. III. Title.

PZ7.P27653Ul 2014

[Fic]—dc23

2013028262

10 9 8 7 6 5 4

LSC-C

Printed in the United States of America

For Matthew, Lucas, and Olivia Morrissey;
Rebecca, Rachel, Andrew, and Alexander Klein;
and all those who, through their generosity,
help get kids reading.
—J.P.

Thanks to Neil, Laura, and most of all Claire.
—A.L.

DON'T LISTEN TO GEORGIA— YOU'VE BEEN WARNED!

Listen to Georgia at your own risk! Trust me — I say this from experience. I have the battle scars to prove it. She's two years younger than I am, so what does she know? This contest is going to be a cakewalk — for ME.

Welcome to the book version of a Doomsday Cage Match. My sister and I are going to go at it mano a mano, which, I'm told, means "hand to hand," not "man to man." Fine. Whatever. Thanks for the vocab lesson, Georgia. (*Not.*) She may have the book smarts in the family, but I'm way funnier. My point is, Georgia will lose this thing the second she opens her mouth. So over to you, Georgia Peach.

Oops, I almost forgot something important. Georgia and I agreed (can you believe it?) that we want YOU to be in the story too. So you get to talk, draw, play a couple of games, do whatever you want. This is YOUR book. Plus, your whole class, your whole school, can join in if they're in the mood. Even teachers!

PLEASE LISTEN TO THE VOICE OF REASON AND SANITY

My motto has always been "MY BROTHER IS A BIG, FAT LIAR!"

In this book, Rafe and I will give our honest opinions on various aspects of middle school life. Like so many of my role models—Gandhi, Oprah Winfrey, Martin Luther King Jr., Hillary Clinton, Barbara Bush, and Mister Rogers—I believe in the importance of friendly dialogue.

In a good, fair debate, you respect your opponent's intelligence, and you should walk away from the experience having learned something new about yourself...unless you're "dialoguing" with an idiot like my brother. Then you just have to prove how unbelievably dumb he is. Talk about easy!

And of course, I'm *really* looking forward to your opinions and anything you'd like to draw. That's why there are all

3

sorts of fun activity pages up ahead. Trust me, though: Rafe couldn't care less what you think. Seriously. He won't even understand most of it.

By the way, I thought up the book's title, though Rafe claims he did. What do you think? You don't have to like it. I do.

MY title

Also, it was my idea to put in all YOUR stuff. I'm looking out for you! Rafe isn't!

MY YEAR—IN GRIEF

The life of a middle schooler is really hard. Am I right? Most definitely. On a month-to-month basis, here's what my year looks like.

SEPTEMBER: Back to school, aka my worst nightmare.

OCTOBER: All memory of summer vacation has been stripped from my brain, thanks to nonstop teacher torture. Halloween candy helps, but only a little.

NOVEMBER: Feels like forever until Christmas vacation. Plus, turkey is not my favorite food, especially when it's served with Georgia's jiggly cranberry jelly.

DECEMBER: Teachers load up on homework and tests before Christmas vacation. Mom listens to the "All Rudolph All the Time" radio station in the car.

JANUARY: I stay up late to watch the New Year's ball squash the very last of my vacation, and fall asleep in class for the next week. Teachers decide to yell their lessons for the rest of the year.

FEBRUARY: HVMS gets all gooey over Valentine's Day, and Mom makes me give out cards to everyone in my class. I get approximately two valentines back.

MARCH: Spring break turns into "spring cleaning time," which means if I sit down even once the whole vacation, I'm not "pitching in."

Please help the valentine-less.

APRIL: Rain. No matter what I do—raincoat, umbrella, galoshes—I get soaked going to school and soaked coming home from school.

MAY: Flowers everywhere make me sneeze. Also, bees. They're after me.

JUNE: FREEDOM!!! Except now there's nothing to do and I'm stuck in the house all day with Georgia.

JULY: Is it possible for a person to sweat to death?

AUGUST: Wait in horror for school to start, while Mom and Georgia get way too excited about buying school supplies and dorky clothes.

GEORGIA

MY TURN: THE ONLY CALENDAR WORTH LOOKING AT

Try a little optimism, Rafe! Here's my calendar:

SEPTEMBER: Hurray! Time to start learning and seeing my friends again!

OCTOBER: Hurray! I'm getting used to my new classes! Can't wait to put together my Georgia O'Keeffe Halloween costume, complete with awesome cattle skull mask! (Search for O'Keeffe's skull paintings on the Internet if you don't know what I'm talking about—it's worth it!)

NOVEMBER: Hurray! It's Thanksgiving and I get to make delicious food with Mom! Everybody *loves* my cranberry jelly rings!

DECEMBER: Hurray! Time for the holidays! Plus, I get to kick butt at end-of-semester tests!

JANUARY: Hurray! Back to school after break! Get to write

the new year's number on all my homework!

FEBRUARY: Hurray! Maybe I'll get a valentine from Sam!

MARCH: Hurray! It's almost spring, which means cleaning out and color-coordinating my closet!

APRIL: Hurray! Midterm reports show that I have all A's!

MAY: Hurray! Time to schedule summer enrichment programs and activities!

JUNE: Hurray! Vacation is here, and I can finally get a jump start on summer reading so I'm *extra* prepared for September!

JULY: Hurray! Fireworks and carnival food for Fourth of July!

AUGUST: Hurray! Shopping for school supplies and new school clothes!

Hurray, hurray, hurray!
So...was that a little too much?
Yeah, I thought so.

YOUR YEAR

You heard our takes on the calendar.
Now it's your turn!

Fill in the boxes with what you love and hate about each month.

APRIL FOOLS' DAY—
BEST HOLIDAY EVER!

I love April Fools' Day, don't you? Only problem is, it's so hard to prank anybody on April Fools'. They're always expecting it! That's why I'm trying to get April Fools' Day switched to August 15.

It's perfect—because no one will suspect any pranks. And August doesn't have any holidays of its own, except, of course, National Toasted Marshmallow Day. So spread the word about the NEW August 15 Fools' Day—just *not* to my mom and sister. I've got some totally great pranks lined up for them.

MY TURN: RAFE'S THE APRIL FOOL HERE!

Rafe is so BUSTED! Why would he write that where he knew I'd see it? Nice try, Rafe, but you'll have to work a little harder than that to put one over on *this* girl. This August, I'm going to be watching you like a hawk watching...well, whatever it is hawks watch like a hawk.

Just wait till April Fools' Day, Rafe. I'm going to pull off a prank so big, even knowing it's April Fools' Day won't stop you from falling for it.

GEORGIA

APRIL (OR AUGUST) FOOLERY

Unscramble the letters to make words related to April Fools' Day. Then unscramble all the letters in the circles to answer the question at the bottom of the page!

AKPRN   _ ◯◯◯ _

SJKEO   _ _ ◯◯ _

RCKIT   _ ◯◯◯ _

RJETSE   _ _ _ ◯ _ _

LUGAH   _ ◯ _ _ ◯

XOHA   ◯◯◯ _

NFU   ◯ _ _

DALEMSI   _ _ _ _ _ ◯◯

16

Who is the biggest fool in the world and probably the universe?

— — — —

— — — — — — — — — — — — — —

(Yes, Georgia wrote this word scramble.)

OH, THE PRINCIPALS I HAVE KNOWN!

And then, uh, study more, and, you know, scholastic aptitude, core curriculum, and other big words! How about *onomatopoeia*? Or *pretentious*?

Being a school principal doesn't seem all that hard to me. All they have to do is wear nicer clothes than the rest of the teachers and decide whether to give you one or two days of detention. Then, every once in a while, they have to speak at a school assembly. Judging by those speeches, they don't exactly take very long to write.

Quite frankly, I don't think

some principals (I won't name names, like Mr. Clarence Dwight, for example) are qualified to say how much detention I should be getting. I think my detention should be determined by a jury of my peers.

MY TURN: PRINCIPALS RAFE HAS KNOWN AND TORTURED

Being a principal doesn't sound so easy to me, especially if you're unlucky enough to have Rafe in your school. From what I hear, Rafe's principal spends most of his time dealing with Rafe. My brother can't figure out how to keep himself from getting into trouble, which makes me wonder...how would Rafe keep ANOTHER Rafe in line?

20

If Rafe were principal, everyone would think it was okay to act like him. Then you'd have a whole school full of Rafes. I don't think the world could handle that.

THE GETTYSBURG ADDRESS (HEY, YOU MIGHT ACTUALLY LEARN SOMETHING HERE)

I HATE memorizing things! There's no point to it. I just forget everything a few days after we have to recite it in class. So this time, here's what I'd like to say for our Gettysburg Address assignment:

Four days and seven hours ago (roughly), our teacher brought forth in this classroom an assignment, conceived in hatred of all things fun, and dedicated to the proposition that middle school students have nothing better to do than sit around memorizing speeches.

If I didn't already know Mom would ground me for the big fat F I'd get, I might actually say that.

WHAT'S THE LONGEST THING YOU'VE HAD TO MEMORIZE? DO YOU STILL REMEMBER IT?

_____

_____

_____

_____

GEORGIA

MY TURN: LET'S HAVE SOME RESPECT FOR HISTORY, RAFE

Now for a more reasonable response to the topic of the Gettysburg Address!

Personally, I like memorizing speeches. I'm very good at it, so it's an easy way to impress a teacher who might not be 100 percent Team Georgia yet, like Ms. Bianca Whitney Matthews. The longer the speech, the longer the teacher stays impressed.

Why, Georgia, I didn't know how brilliant you were! I'll take this into account when grading your papers for the rest of the school year.

If I had to rewrite the Gettysburg Address, however, this is what I'd say:

Four days and seven arguments ago, our mother brought forth on our living room a new rule, conceived poorly, and dedicated to the terrible idea that I should vacuum EVERY afternoon.

Now we are engaged in a great civil war, testing whether this girl, or any girl, so opposed to housework and with so many better things to do, can long endure such unnecessary vacuuming.

So what do you think? Who spoofed it better? (I deserve extra points because I did two sentences.)

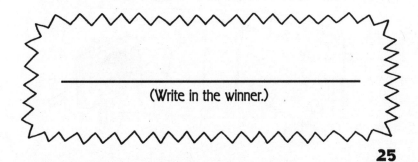

(Write in the winner.)

FIELD TRIPS ARE BOGUS!

Every kid looks forward to field trips, right?
Wrong. Why are they even called *field* trips? Over
the years, lots of my teachers have taken us to the
world's most boring museum, or a ball-bearing
factory, or a courthouse, or an aquarium that was
half-closed because of a couple of leaky tanks.
Man, you could smell the green aquarium slime
and fish poop from the parking lot.

But not once have the teachers taken us to a field. What's that all about? You think if they say "field" they're going to take us to watch a baseball or football game, right? Or at least let us play by ourselves in a field and give us some Kool-Aid and watermelon and hot dogs while they're at it. But none of that has anything to do with field trips. They're really just forced marches around places that have parking spaces for school buses.

MY TURN: RAFE'S OUT IN LEFT FIELD (AS USUAL)

Rafe never wants to go to school, even when it's in a classroom. If they took him to a field, he'd probably have something to say about that too—too sunny, too cold, too grassy, too *fieldish*— or something equally Rafe-ian.

Besides, what are we going to learn in a field? How slowly grass grows? What color dirt is? Some of us are trying to get an education so that one day we can get fancy jobs and our older brothers will be working for *us*!

How did this happen?

You lost the showdown big-time, remember? Now empty the wastebasket, brother dear.

THE BOSS

GEORGIA

LiBRARiAN RAGe
(HeY, IT HAPPeNS!)

Most librarians I've met are super-sweet, but there's this one who seriously has it in for me. She's so fussy about me taking out too many books at once, and she's constantly trying to keep me from taking out books that she *thinks* are above my reading level. What did I ever do to her? Well, okay, a few things.

Here's how to make a librarian hate you.

1. SPILL YOUR DRINK ON A BOOK YOU BORROWED.

2. ASK FOR OBSCURE BOOKS THAT THE LIBRARIAN HAS TO TAKE TIME TO SPECIAL-ORDER FROM ANOTHER LIBRARY.

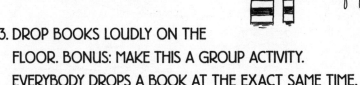

3. DROP BOOKS LOUDLY ON THE FLOOR. BONUS: MAKE THIS A GROUP ACTIVITY. EVERYBODY DROPS A BOOK AT THE EXACT SAME TIME.

(Who says I'm a Goody Two-Shoes now?)

GEORGIA

ALL HAiL THE KEEPERS OF GOOD BOOKS!

Let's face it, a librarian can have a big impact on your boredom level in school by recommending the perfect book for how you're feeling...OR forcing you to read the encyclopedia during library hour. So here's a chance to guarantee that your school librarian likes you and— BONUS—feels really good. Fill in this bookmark and slip it into a book you're returning so that your librarian is sure to see it. (Don't forget to let your mom and dad see it too. Parents love this kind of stuff.)

Oh, that is so nice of you. You can borrow as many books as you want. Don't even bother to return them.

LIBRARIANS:
THE ORIGINAL SEARCH ENGINES!
SEES ALL!
KNOWS ALL!
MIDDLE SCHOOL
Why I LOVE my librarian:

MY TURN: ON THE FLIP SIDE...

Whoa. Wait a second. If Miss Goody Two-Shoes gets to do a bookmark, I do too.

I mean, seriously, do we really need official "bookmarks" to mark where we are in a book? That's what old napkins are for. Or those sticky-note dealios. You can even use a spare spork from KFC.

> Now you know why they call her a Goody Two-Shoes!

> Hey, sometimes it gets so bad I call her a Goody Two-THOUSAND-Shoes.

But if you must have a bookmark, cut out this page. You can glue it to the back of the sappy one you did on Georgia's page. (But maybe you shouldn't show this side to your parents. Just a thought.)

BOOKMARKS LIKE THIS ONE ARE A DUMB AND STUPID IDEA

I could've used ANYTHING to mark where I was in this book. A scrap of paper. A straw from the cafeteria. Just the straw wrapper. I could've used an old sock! Do we really need special slips of paper to remind us where we stopped reading? Think of all the trees we could save. And paper cuts we could avoid. Don't get me started on paper cuts! Bookmarks should be on your Web browser, not sticking their noses into your books.

Sincerely,
Rafe Khatchadorian

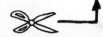

CURSiVE,
I CURSe YOU

Come on. Do we really need to learn *two* different ways to write? One is hard enough. And by the time we're done with learning how to write *exactly* the way our teachers want, we're doing half of our work on computers. Cursive is just another item on my hugely long list of "Things That Waste My Time at School."

A lot of schools don't even teach cursive writing anymore. Mine does, clearly just to torture me. So I pride myself on having *the worst* handwriting in my entire school. *Seriously, the worst!*

My handwriting is sort of like a secret code only I can read. Most of the other kids in my class write in perfect script, drawing their curly *L*s, adding little smiley faces to their *O*s and goofy hearts above their *I*s. Especially Matthew-Lucas Morrissey and his twin sister, Olivia Morrissey. The Morrisseys all have a lot of froufrou letters in their names.

it's so stupid!

But that's not my style. I have a cooler brand of chicken scratch. I call it *Rafe Scratchadorian*.

THE SAD END OF LOCKER DECORATIONS AT OUR SCHOOL

Well, I think it's sad that no one takes cursive seriously anymore. Not only is script handwriting on its way out, but can you believe *this*? My school just banned locker decorations "of any kind." They say they're a fire hazard. Seriously? Has there ever, in the history of lockers, been a locker fire?

I think my school is more intent on banning *happiness* "of any kind" than keeping the school from catching on fire. If they really want to stop fires, they should ban some of our teachers from using so much hair spray. Some of them look ready to erupt. And I know plenty of bullies who would be willing to strike a match close by....

LADIES AND GENTLEMEN, I GIVE YOU THE LOWEST FORM OF LIFE IN MIDDLE SCHOOL: THE BULLY

Bullying doesn't make any sense to me. Bullies always pick on kids who are different. But what's so bad about "different"?

You know what else is different? Detention being held at a movie theater. Waking up and finding school has been canceled, and from now on you get to go to an amusement park every day instead. Lunch will be chips, cotton candy, and corn dogs. That's different. Who would make fun of that?

I WISH EVERY DAY COULD BE **THIS** DIFFERENT!

CLINK
CLINK
CLINK

If you think about it, most kids aren't bullies, which means the bullies themselves are extremely different. If bullies ever took the time to think about it, they'd have to start bullying themselves.

MY TURN:
THE BIGGER PICTURE
ON BULLYING

There are two types of bullies in the world, Rafe, and the way I see it, they haven't changed much throughout history. First, you have your Miller-the-Mini-Killer types. Threatening to beat people up has been bullies' go-to strategy for, like, thousands of years. Maybe longer.

CENTURIES LATER...

But then there's a second kind of bully, like the Princess Patrol (my nickname for a group of girls at school who constantly pick on me). You don't have to worry about physical violence from them—just constant humiliation. We have a special name for those particular kinds of angry people around here: word bullies. Different methods, very similar results. Word bullies can be just as bad as your standard-issue Miller-the-Mini-Killer bullies, plus they can strike anytime, anywhere. (Some grown-ups—even teachers, coaches, and parents—use word-bullying.) And, like the other bully variety, word bullies have had eons to hone their technique.

Did I win this contest yet? I hope so. Maybe that's why my idea got *three* pages. I'm just sayin'.

YOUR TURN TO SPEAK OUT ABOUT BULLIES!

Draw or write about the absolute worst bully you ever met. Go for it!

The next time a bully threatens you, just picture them in their underpants. The kind with puppy dogs and kittens.

WHAT DOES YOUR SCHOOL DO TO STOP BULLIES?

_____

_____

_____

_____

WHAT WOULD YOU DO IF *YOU* WERE IN CHARGE? (MAYBE YOU *SHOULD* BE IN CHARGE, RIGHT?)

_____

_____

_____

_____

HERE'S A TOUGH ONE. HAVE YOU EVER BEEN A BULLY? EVEN A WORD BULLY? MOST OF US PROBABLY HAVE. YOU CAN TELL US ABOUT IT. BONUS POINTS FOR HONESTY!

_____

_____

_____

CAN YOU SPOT WHiCH ONe OF THeSe BULLieS iS DiFFeReNT AND WHY? CiRCLe HiM!

Yep. The one who thinks he's funny but he's SNOT.

Here's something for you to stick
on your locker or book covers or backpack!

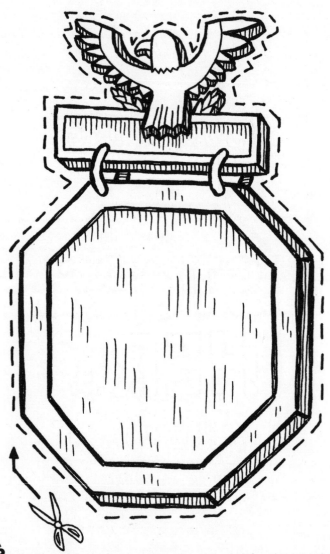

46

HERE'S SOME ROOM TO DRAW ANTI-BULLYING CARTOONS. CHECK MINE OUT!

Big, Lonely Loser
Yearning for Attention

HOW TO OUTRUN A BULLY (SOMETIMES)

If you've ever tried to outrun a bully, then you know it's not easy. Don't worry about it, because I've got some simple tips for you.

TIP 1: GET A HEAD START.

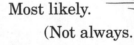

Who is that kid? The Road Runner?

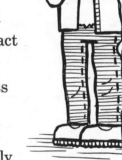

Physically, bullies are big and fast. But their brains are the exact opposite—small and slow. If you start running before they process what's going on, you'll most likely get away.

Most likely.

(Not always.

Okay, I'll be honest—it only worked once.)

TiP 2: AiM FOR FRiENDLY TERRiTORY.

Run near places teachers are known to frequent, like the teachers' lounge, the teachers' parking lot, and snack machines. Just be sure it's obvious you're the victim, or you could get in trouble too. Crying may not be cool, but it helps. Actually, crying usually works. Though maybe not with the other kids.

TiP 3: CONDUCT TRiAL RUNS.

Sometime after school, practice getting away from areas where bullying is frequent and moving to areas that aren't so bad. Like I said, bullies aren't smart. If you make a hard left onto the stairs by the cafeteria, the bully is likely going to slow down while he figures out what stairs are and how to use them.

That ought to do it! Good luck, and stay safe!

PRACTICE MAKES PERFECT

Can you find your way to the Safe Zone before the bully gives you a swirlie or a triple nip-nerf? Remember, bullies mostly go into mazes for the free cheese.

GEORGIA

BULLIES YOU CAN'T OUTRUN

So "someone" recently sent my friend Rhonda a really mean e-mail. Lucky for us, Rhonda read it in the school's computer lab, so I was there to be her shoulder to cry on. Literally. Somebody made my friend cry just because they could.

Here's a tip, cyberbullies: If you're going to send someone a nasty e-mail, be sure to send it from an e-mail address that has your name in it so we know who to fear! (Rafe was right—bullies are about as sharp as a bowling ball.)

I didn't send it.

:SNIFF:

GRRR!

It came from Missy.Trillin@MacNCheesyohs.com.

That could have been anyone.

SCHOOL DANCES ARE SCAAARRRY!

Last night, I did the unthinkable. I went to a school dance. It was just as horrible as it sounds. No, there weren't monsters or ghouls or zombies. I wish there had been, actually. That would've been cool.

Instead, there was dancing. Including *slow* dancing. And, well, I suppose I'll have to tell you this sooner or later: It turns out I can't dance. And I don't just mean I'm not particularly good at dancing. I mean I literally do *not* possess the ability to dance. I can't even shuffle from side to side without stumbling over my own feet. They nearly had to call 911. And I owe the school a new punch bowl.

53

GEORGIA

MY TURN: NO WONDER RAFE CAN'T DANCE

I hate passing over an attempt to rag on Rafe....

You know what I hate about jam?

The fact that you don't know how to spell it?

But in his defense, boys at middle school dances can *never* dance. It's usually not a big deal, though, because you rarely see them actually hit the dance floor. Most of them spend all night standing against a wall, trying to work up the courage to ask a girl to dance, so all the girls end up dancing with each other in a big clump.

But if Rafe knows he can't dance, that means he actually tried dancing, right? Does that also mean he actually asked someone to dance with him? Did Rafe ask his longtime crush, Jeanne Galletta?

LET'S DANCE!

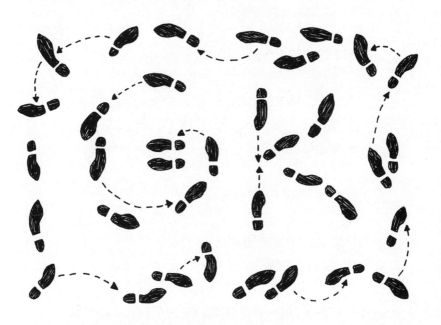

Come up with a cool name for this dance and then practice the steps. Show your friends and family how to do it! Don't forget to pick the perfect song for it.

COOL DANCE NAME:

THE _____

PERFECT SONG FOR THIS DANCE:

_____

57

THE BEST AND WORST

Rate some of the best and worst things about school dances, with 1 being the best and 10 being the worst. You can use our ideas or make up your own!

____ EATING THE JUNK FOOD

____ DANCING LIKE A MANIAC

____ SLOW DANCING

____ BUYING NEW CLOTHES

____ STARING AT THE LINES ON THE GYM FLOOR

____ DANCING WITH THE HERD (SO NOBODY KNOWS WHO YOU'RE DANCING WITH)

____ BURNING YOUR FACE WITH YOUR DAD'S AFTERSHAVE (EVEN THOUGH YOU DON'T SHAVE)

____ WATCHING A TEACHER TRY TO DANCE

____ HELPING TO DECORATE THE GYM (OR WHEREVER THE DANCE IS)

____ DOING A MOONWALK (OR TRYING TO, ANYWAY)

____ BEING ASKED TO DANCE BY THE PERSON YOU'RE CRUSHING ON

____ MAKING UP A NEW DANCE CALLED THE ZOMBIE JERK

____ GULPING SUGARY DRINKS YOU DON'T GET AT HOME

____ LOOKING LIKE A FOOL

RAFE

HOW TO DO THE CHICKEN DANCE THE NEXT TIME ONE OF YOUR RELATIVES GETS MARRIED

1. The second you hear the first chicken cheeps, run to the dance floor and join the circle.

2. Hold both arms up in front of you, and make two "beaks" with your hands. Open and close your beaks four times to the music. (Do not attack people with your beaks.)

THHB!

PFBT!

Moooooom !!!

3. Put your thumbs in your armpits and flap your elbows four times to the music. (If you can pop off an armpit fart, give yourself bonus points.)

4. Bend your knees and wiggle your hips four times to the music, placing your arms and hands behind your butt like the tail feathers of a chicken.

5. Straighten your knees and clap four times, with the music. (Chickens do this for exercise.)

6. Repeat steps 2 through 5 four times.

7. Join hands with the person on each side of you (unless it's your sister) and skip around in a circle to the music, reversing the direction of the circle once. (Most people will not be able to figure this out—just go with it.)

8. Repeat the entire sequence until the song ends or you die of embarrassment, whichever comes first.

Don't have a wedding coming up? Try it in math class and see what happens!

PRINCIPAL'S OFFICE

A FIGHT WITH THE FLOOR

No, my nose is not a result of me falling against a wall laughing at Rafe attempting to do the chicken dance. And I didn't get into a

fight at school, even though Mom thinks I did. Who does she think I am—Rafe?

I was walking down the stairs at school and not paying attention to where I was going, and I fell. Flat on my face. Bloody nose and everything.

It was super-embarrassing, but when I got home Mom wouldn't believe me. It does look a lot like someone punched me, but now she's calling all my teachers, trying to find out what happened! This is a nightmare!

Hold on. I honestly can't believe what just happened....

Rafe just stuck up for me. He heard the truth from a kid who actually saw me fall. And he told Mom what happened. I wonder what he's up to?

I guess I have to fess up: I'm just kind of clumsy. So I guess Rafe and I do have *something* in common.

It was hilarious. You should have been there, Mom!

Heh
Heh
Heh

DRESS CODE: TWO WORDS THAT STRIKE TERROR IN ME!

Of all the stupid rules that schools have, the dress code is the most ridiculous. Yes, I get that we can't go to school naked, but school policy should end there. If you're wearing clothes, you should be golden.

What's wrong with what I'm wearing?

TAP
TAP
TAP

Why do they have to add on so many restrictions? What is the problem with kids wearing sunglasses at school? They're not dark enough to make me trip over anything. And it's not like they're a really effective disguise or anything. I don't know what the celebrities are thinking.

And if the school doesn't want me to wear jeans with holes in them, I suggest they give me some money to go buy new jeans!

GEORGIA

MY TURN: HERE'S A SHOCKER— I DISAGREE WITH RAFE

I hate your skirt.

A dress code would be awesome! And you know what? I'm even in favor of school uniforms. That way there wouldn't be any competition about clothes. That would be so refreshing. Then Missy Trillin, the alpha female of the Princess Patrol at HVMS, couldn't make fun of my clothes, because we'd be wearing the same thing!

You took the words right out of my mouth!

But I guess she'd still be able to make fun of my hair...and jewelry...and makeup. Even if the school *made* us style all those things completely the same, I'm positive she'd still find something to pick on.

Your eyebrows are so drab. How can you even leave home in the morning?

My mom forces me.

ROCK YOUR STYLE

Okay, here's where you say anything you want about dress codes! Does your school have one? If not, would a dress code be a good or terrible thing at your school? Tell us why you think so.

_____

_____

_____

_____

CIRCLE THE THREE BEST ITEMS TO WEAR TO SCHOOL. (THEN SEE WHAT YOUR FRIENDS PICKED!)

NEW JEANS

CUTE FLATS

BANGLES

BUTTON-DOWN SHIRT

FUNNY T-SHIRT

JEGGINGS

FOOTBALL JERSEY

SKATER SHOES

SHORTS

SKINNY BELT

KHAKIS

HOOP EARRINGS

POLO SHIRT

COOL KICKS

RATTY HOODIE

FLIP-FLOPS

CARGO PANTS   CARDIGAN
CORDUROYS   TULLE SKIRT
PEACE SIGNS   FLANNEL SHIRT
UGGS   CASUAL SKIRT
SKINNY JEANS   OLD JEANS

CIRCLE THE THREE WORST.

TIE AND WHITE SHIRT   MASK AND CAPE
SWEATER VEST   PRINCESS SPARKLE COSTUME
FEDORA   THREE-PIECE SUIT
PLAID PANTS   BRIGHT ORANGE CROCS
SEQUINED ANYTHING   JEWELED JEANS
BALLERINA TUTU   GYM UNIFORM
TURTLENECK   SWEATER
BLAZER WITH CREST   GRAPHIC POLO
ON POCKET   WITH DRAGON ON IT

That is NOT in the dress code!

HELP MY BROTHER— PLEASE

Rafe isn't much on colorful clothing. He's an artist. They wear a lot of black. So here's our chance. Grab your colored pencils or markers and let's give Rafe some color. You can give him polka dots too. Even a mustache. Hey, they're your markers—let yourself go. Be, you know, like Rafe—super-artistic!

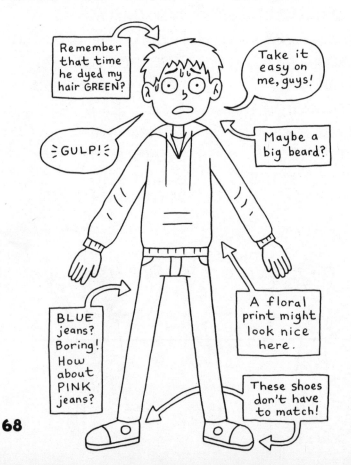

HOW TO BREAK IN A PAIR OF JEANS

Seems like just when I have a pair of jeans exactly the way I want them, my mom throws them out and buys me a new pair. She thinks pants should look crisp and clean all the time.

But everybody (except maybe Georgia) knows jeans aren't even ready until you've worn them for a hundred days without washing, climbed at least five trees while wearing them, and worn a hole in the knee so your leg can breathe. Moms need to understand that it's not until your pants are being held together by safety pins and duct tape that you should even consider getting a new pair.

YOUR TAKE ON CLOTHES!

ROCK ON!

Fill in your answers and then see what your friends said.

Are clothes important or overrated?

_____

Where do you buy your clothes?

_____

What clothes do you want to add to your wardrobe next?

_____

CUTE AND COMFY

How many pairs of jeans are in your closet right now?

_____

What colors look best on you?

_____

Are name brands worth the extra cost?

_____

What's your best clothes-shopping secret?

_____

What's trendy right now?

_____

What do you think will be trendy next year?

_____

If you could start a fashion trend, what would it be?

_____

Parental units' fashion sense—good, bad, or awful?

_____

What's one thing only old people wear?

_____

What was the dumbest thing you wore two years ago?

_____

Who is the class fashionista in your grade?

_____

Is your closet organized or a disaster zone?

_____

What do you wear when you sleep?

_____

CASUAL AND COOL

Only I could make this look good!

Is there any hope for Rafe's warped sense of fashion?

_____

Can Georgia rock any look?

_____

BODY ODOR—
JUST A THEORY

Some of the kids in my class are clearly in denial about their body odor. Our classrooms smell so bad, some days I think I'll throw up. No wonder I fail a math test every once in a while, when it feels like I've got dirty socks stuffed up my nose!

I think this is a metaphor. Maybe a simile. Not totally sure. Ask your teacher.

Thomas Edison might've said "Genius is one percent inspiration and ninety percent perspiration," but the guy didn't exactly invent the lightbulb surrounded by a bunch of sweaty middle school kids!

Mom! We're all out of breakfast deodorant!

It's not like deodorant is hard to put on. Do these kids mess up and put it on their face by accident? Or slather it on their morning toast? I don't think I even want to know!

GEORGIA

MY TURN: LOOK WHO'S TALKiNG ABOUT B.O.

I'd settle for Rafe using any deodorant at all. He totally doesn't, so it's pretty outrageous to hear him complaining about everyone else. Or maybe whatever he *is* using just isn't strong enough to mask that "I've been rolling around in garbage all day" smell, which is why I've perfected the art of breathing through my mouth around him. I've tried leaving my own stick on his dresser with a Post-it note that says "TRY ME" on it, but he's not taking the hint.

Here's what I don't get: Why are girls supposed to use different deodorant than boys? What would happen if a boy used a girl's deodorant? Would he suddenly turn into a girl?

Obviously, that wouldn't happen, so it's totally just some ploy to get twice as many people to buy deodorant. If you think Rafe should get with the program and just use my deodorant (or buy his own), e-mail him (again and again, please)!

75

A THOUSAND AND ONE BAD HAIR DAYS

Mom always—like every single day before school—tells me my hair looks scruffy. Messy. Greasy. Unkempt (whatever that means). But it's not my fault. I'd take better care of my hair if she'd let me get a cool hairstyle. I think I would look so awesome with a Mohawk.

How do people keep these things up?

You think bullies bother a kid with a Mohawk? Of course not! But I'm not picky. I would happily settle for dreadlocks. Or a shaved head. Or better yet, a head that's almost entirely shaved except for my name spelled out with my hair.

Cool. Very cool.

Good thing he didn't misspell it!

HELP RAFE FIND
HIS NEW DO!

Circle your fave. Cross out your least favorite!

GEORGIA

MY TURN: I CAN'T BELIEVE RAFE BROUGHT UP HAIR

Are you kidding me, Rafe? You once tricked me into dyeing my hair GREEN, and it didn't wash out for DAYS! Now you have the nerve to whine about Mom wanting you to comb your perfectly normal-colored hair every once in a while? Seriously—it would take me less than five seconds.

> Five... four...three... two...one!

To be fair, people at school, like Rebecca and Rachel Klein, ended up thinking my green hair was kind of awesome. So I decided not to put purple dye in Rafe's body wash...this time. But watch your back, Rafe! That's always a possibility. And somehow I don't think you can pull off *purple skin* the way I pulled off green hair.

HA HA HA HA HA

AAAAHHH!!! I look like Barney the dinosaur!

FREE PERIOD

This is a free period. Repeat—free period—to do anything you want. Write, rant, doodle, or use the book as a cool pillow to grab a quick nap. It's up to you!

FREE PERIOD

FREE PERIOD

THE BiZARRO-RANT

By now, I guess you're all getting used to my rant procedure: I pick out something I don't like and tell you why. Well, this time the thing that's making me most angry is a kid named Rafe.

> Nice going, Rafe. I suspected you might be partially human.

That's right, me. Here's why I'm mad at myself: Today I saw Tommy Francis throw Joey Garcia's backpack out the window, and I didn't do anything about it. What does that make me? A co-bully? Even after being bullied so much myself, all I could do was stand there and watch, like it was a TV show.

I know it's not my fault Joey was being bullied, but I still should have done *something*.

> Man, what's wrong with that Rafe kid?

> I'm YOU, dummy!

RAFE'S OFFICIAL FART CHART (THIS IS A CLASSIC, TRUST ME)

All right, people. On a much less serious note, it's time for what I would say is probably the most excellent part of this book, of course written by me. It will change everything you thought you knew about bodily noises. Are you ready for a truth bomb? Here it is:

Most people (especially adults) think a fart is just a fart.

But I, through years of nose-stinging research, have a flowchart for the kinds of farts I personally think exist.

I take back what I just said about my brother being partially human.

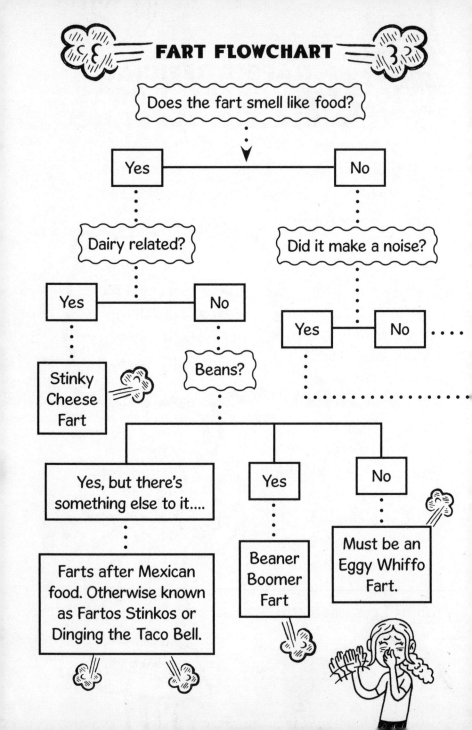

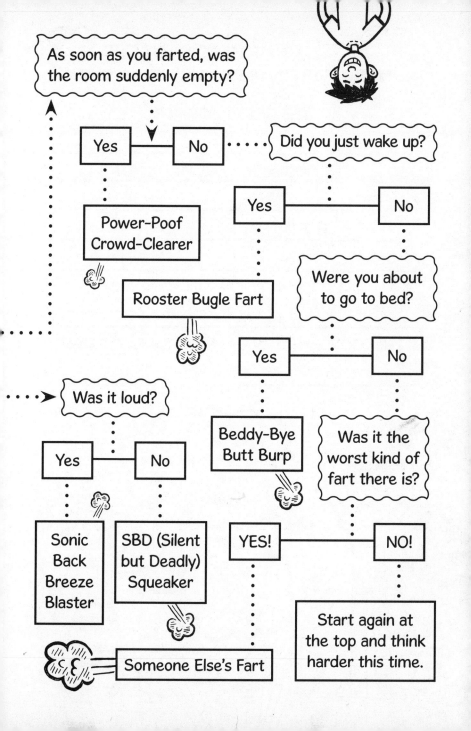

MORE FART NAMES: ADD YOUR OWN!

THE SILENT STINKER

THE SOCIALLY AWKWARD TOOT

THE INTESTINE CLENCHER

THE POPCORN POPPER IN YOUR PANTS

THE "OOPS, THAT WASN'T JUST A FART" FART

POPPING ZITS!

Oh, good, Georgia's left me alone, so I can rant about my biology teacher, Mrs. Herkimer, who's always saying boys don't mature as fast as girls. I always want to call out, in my best, smarmy Georgia voice, "Gender bias! Gender bias!" (which is something that Georgia likes to yell at me in front of Mom all the time). But I keep my mouth shut because I am, regardless of what the Herkimer says, mature. (Also, I'm scared to death of the Herkimer.)

Okay, so I'm about to prove Mrs. H. wrong. You ready?

It's been my experience that girls love popping each other's zits.

Gross, right? And you *know* it's true, Georgia. So do your pals in your band (which is called We Stink, by the way, because they stink).

So how's that for maturity, Mrs. Herkimer?

Boo!

Excellent— Georgia's still hiding in her room trying to forget about my incredible Fart Chart, which means she can't respond to my obviously true point that girls are as immature as boys. And zits are even grosser than farts—it's a fact.

Wait a minute—Jamie Grimm? From *I Funny*? That whole book was hilarious. I actually read it. Three times!

Did someone say farts? Zits? I've got a really cool zit joke, actually.

So are you going to tell us a totally disgusting zit joke?

Can't. Too gross. Don't want your sister to get on my case.

Then you pretty much can't tell ANY jokes. Except maybe a joke about a teacup!

No problem! At my middle school the science teacher has a very simple test for intelligence. She fills a bathtub with water and then offers you a spoon, a teacup, and a bucket to empty the tub. Which one would you pick to show how smart you are?

Easy. The bucket, because it's bigger than the spoon or the teacup!

True. But if you were really smart, you'd just empty the tub by pulling out the drain plug.

Hold it, Jamie. I can't work under this kind of pressure! Who sent you here? Was it Georgia?

Rafe, call me when you get your nerves under control. I already choke enough for both of us!

Bye! You funny!

Wow. Jamie Grimm of *I Funny*, right here inside our book, watching me think!

(Uh-oh. I totally just set Georgia up for saying something snarky about me "thinking," so I'd better get another activity in before she realizes it's her turn!)

HOW TO ARMPIT FART

1. Cup your hand. If you're a righty, use your right hand. If you're a lefty, use your left.

2. Open your opposite armpit by raising your elbow.

3. Put your hand cup side up under the open armpit.

4. Lower your arm and push down.

EXTRA POINTS FOR DURATION, HIGH DECIBEL LEVEL, AND PUMPING OUT RECOGNIZABLE TUNES.

91

NO PiERCiNGS FOR Me, THANK YOU VeRY MUCH

Okay, *anybody* with half a boring brain can do fart jokes. I guess Rafe just proved that.

So now I guess I'm *forced* to beat him at his own game. So listen to this: For the past two years, I've been begging Mom to let me get pierced ears. Well, that stops today.

A girl in my math class got her ears pierced over the weekend, and one ear got infected. It was the most disgusting thing I have seen in my entire life, and remember, my brother is Rafe.

Her ear was as swollen and purple as a moldy grape, and she had this white stuff oozing out of the hole in her ear that looked like soggy spaghetti.

What?!

But who will make your ears extra sparkly?

Is Georgia afraid of a teensy-weensy prick on the earlobe?

Sorry, pretty earrings, but you will never be mine. I think I'll definitely be a tattoo kind of girl.

GEORGIA

SO...WHO'S WINNING AT THE HALF?

All right, friends. You're about halfway through this book, and I think it's pretty clear who's made their arguments the best. I even stooped so low as to beat Rafe at his own "gross" game with my genius (if I do say so myself) section about pierced ears.

In your dreams! I'm kicking butt so far, and everybody knows it. Did you see my stuff about outrunning bullies? I'm providing a useful service here.

Let's ask them for their predictions, then, if you're so confident.

Fine. But remember that it's not over until the flat lady sinks!

It's "until the FAT lady SINGS," genius.

That right there should put me in first place. But tell us what you think! Fill in below who's winning so far, and then keep reading!

_____
(winner so far)

THE WORLD-FAMOUS TOMMY TUNA

Mention the words *tuna fish* and I'll barf on you. I almost just did. Know why? Tommy Tuna Ackerman. Every day since kindergarten, Tommy Tuna shows up with a bag lunch speckled with tuna fish stains.

Forgot... my... gas... mask...

Every class has a smelly tuna kid, but if there were a Smelly Kid Olympics, Tommy would take home more gold than Michael Phelps. For years this kid has sacrificed his social life for his love of tuna. Tuna sandwiches, tuna pancakes, tuna casseroles, tuna tacos—Tommy probably has tuna ice cream after din-din. Show him a surface and he'll smear it with tuna and eat it.

You can actually see tuna vapors coming out of his pores. And when Tommy lifts his arms...poof! A tuna mist shoots out of his armpits and hovers over the class like a San Francisco fog. Time to put on my gas mask and run, or I'll be late for class. One whiff of that tuna and who knows how many periods I could miss in the nurse's office.

RAFe'S NO GeRMOPHOBE

First of all, Rafe should lose about fifty points right there because making fun of Tommy Ackerman is *totally* being a word bully—completely inappropriate, Rafe! Second, I can't believe Rafe is so super-sensitive about bad smells. Have you seen his room? He's harvesting bacteria. It's like a petri dish in there!

I had to stop drinking milk because he's always drinking it straight out of the carton. Now I'm probably gonna get osteoporosis from not getting enough calcium. Because of him!

Beware, Rafe! From now on I will be replacing the milk in the carton with something disgusting, and you won't know until it hits your tongue. You've been warned!

By the way, reader, I'm now warning you that the next few pages are SERIOUSLY vomitizing!

WHAT DID THE KID WITH THE STOMACH VIRUS HAVE FOR LUNCH?

Cut out, mount on cardboard or foam core,
and show your Gross-Out Pride!

DR. RAFE'S OFFICIAL BURP DIAGNOSIS (ALSO A CLASSIC)

Did you think my Fart Chart was helpful? I hope so. Actually, I *know* so. I'll bet you're ready for a bonus—so here's a handy list of questions to help you diagnose your burps!

Was it something you ate?••••••• | Yes.

Did it come from a drive-thru window? ••• | Yes.

Fast-Food McBurp? •••• | Some of it might have been....

Overeating Binge Burp? •••••• | I hadn't eaten anything in hours!

Something you drank? ••••••••• | Yes.

Soda Gas Bubbler Burp? · · · · · · · · · No.

Milk Shake Belly Quake Belch? · · · · · · · · Nope.

Were you about to throw up? · · · · · · Yes.

Pre-Upchuck Burp-Up? · · · · · · · · · · · · · · No.

Did you just finish throwing up? · · · · · · Yes.

Post-Hurl, Last-Urp Burp? · · · · · · · · · · · · · · No.

Can you still taste
the burp? · · · · · · · Yes.

Flavor Savor Burp? · · · · No.

Can you imagine actually living with this guy? 24/7, 365 × 10? No. You cannot.

106

Any chance it was something else?･･･････

Maybe…not 100 percent sure. This is getting tricky.

Might be a hiccup?･････････

Nope, took me completely by surprise.

What did it sound like?･････････････

The end of the world.

Monster Burp?･･･････････

No. At the end of the world, everything's quiet.

Ah! A silent burp?･･･････････････

Yeah!

OKAY. GOT IT. IT WAS AN UPSIDE-DOWN FART!

THE GREAT BREAKFAST/DINNER DEBATE

Let's get back to basics here and talk about a burp's delicious beginnings: food! It's one of my favorite topics. But I'm seriously annoyed about one thing: If I want pancakes at dinnertime, what's wrong with that? If I want a burger for breakfast, why would anyone try to stop me? But restaurants stop serving breakfast at eleven, and when I make fish sticks on a Saturday morning, Mom gives me a funny look.

I think it's a conspiracy. Someone is trying to force us to eat certain foods at certain times. I haven't figured out who's behind it yet, but they're benefiting from no one eating waffles past noon!

Whoever you are, know this—I'm onto you! Also, it's seven at night, and I'm eating a bagel. With bacon! Take THAT!

WHAT'S YOUR FAVORITE BREAKFAST FOOD TO EAT AT THE "WRONG" TIME OF DAY?

MY TURN:
RAFE'S CONSPIRACY
THEORY IS BALONEY!

Listen, Rafe, if I catch you trying to talk Mom into making waffles for dinner one more time, I'm throwing the waffle iron out the window (after first checking to make sure there are no innocent passersby outside, of course). Breakfast food tastes best in the morning. Orange juice is full of sunny citrus, and fried eggs look like the sun, both of which make you alert and ready to face the day. Eat that stuff at night and you'll be too wired to go to bed. And we can't have dinner food for breakfast, because dinner food takes so long to cook.

I don't want Mom to have to wake up before sunrise to get the meat loaf in the oven.

Just accept it, Rafe: Breakfast food is best for breakfast, and dinner food is best for dinner. End of discussion.

WHO DO YOU AGREE WITH? (ME, RIGHT?)

RAFE'S BEST DINNER MENU EVER

Need some ideas for dinner tonight? Find and circle a few of my faves! Look for words up, down, forward, backward, or diagonally.

WORD LIST

PANCAKES

BISCUITS

WAFFLES

DONUTS

FRENCH TOAST

MUFFINS

CINNAMON BUNS

CEREAL

BACON

COLD PIZZA

SAUSAGE

HAMBURGERS

113

BRUSSELS: CURSED CITY OF THE SPROUT

I hope I get a chance to travel all around the world one day, but you know where I never need to go? Brussels.

I'm sure there are lots of little things growing in the ground there that won't quite kill you, but seriously, I just couldn't trust the food in Brussels.

I mean, they decided to name their city after the worst-tasting vegetable in the entire world....It can't be good for tourism!

WHAT ARE YOUR LEAST FAVORITE FOODS IN THE WHOLE WORLD?

_____

_____

_____

FOOD FiGHT

What's the best food in the world? Make a choice and move it on to the next round!

PIZZA

BURGER

TACO

NACHOS

ICE CREAM

CAKE

SLIDER

HOT DOG

SPAGHETTI

MAC & CHEESE

FRIED CHICKEN

FRENCH FRIES

PANCAKES

MASHED POTATOES

PB & J

BOLOGNA

Nom Nom Nom

↑ FINALS!

↑ SEMI-FINALS

↑ QUARTER FINALS

↑ GREAT 8

↑ SWEET 16

munch munch munch

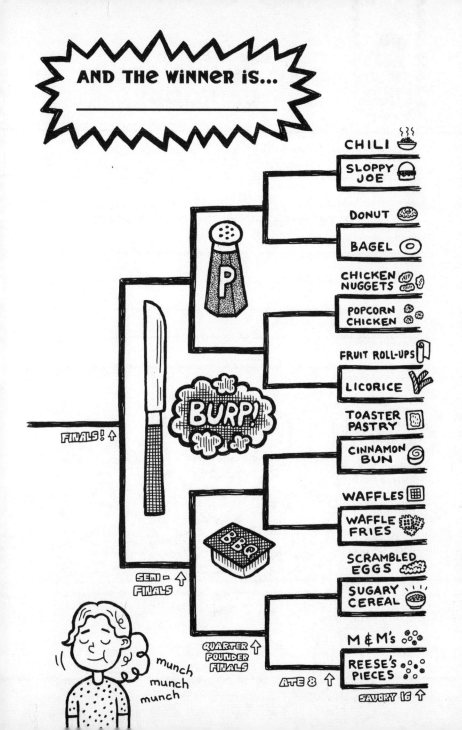

GIVE US THE SCOOP ON FOOD!

What should your school's cafeteria serve for lunch tomorrow?

WRITE WHAT YOU REALLY WANT!

_____

_____

_____

_____

_____

If you could replace your cafeteria with a fast-food restaurant, which one would you choose?

☐ McDonald's
☐ KFC
☐ Taco Bell
☐ Burger King
☐ Pizza Hut

☐ None—I'd want food from that cool diner with the awesome apple pie.

ADD YOUR FAVORITE RESTAURANTS HERE!

_____

_____

_____

AN IMPORTANT MESSAGE ABOUT COOKING—ALSO, BACON!

Thanks to growing up with a mom who loves to cook, I've known how to whip up cupcake batter since I was old enough to reach a counter.

This led to learning how to turn on the stove, which led to learning how to make all kinds of delicious things, like pancakes and stir-fries and my personal favorite: BACON!

So you can see why I almost cried last week when a girl in my Family and Consumer Science class didn't have any idea how to cook bacon. She thought it came in bags all crisped up, like potato chips. First of all—seriously? You've *never* seen someone make bacon?

Second of all—what are you going to do the next time you want to surprise your mom with breakfast in bed?

And finally, when you know how to cook, you can be in charge of making dinner. No gross meat loaf or soggy vegetables. I'm talking about delicious pasta with garlic bread, and cupcakes for dessert.

I rest my case.

Where does bacon come from? Bacon trees? I need to get one!

BACON—IT'S NOT JUST FOR BREAKFAST (AND BURGERS AND PEANUT BUTTER SANDWICHES) ANYMORE!

They say bacon is "meat candy"! That's why there's bacon jerky, bacon pancakes, bacon brittle, bacon popcorn, and bacon lollipops—all very real products. But it's time for some more. Add bacon to any of these and then come up with a cool name for your new product!

ICE CREAM _____

_____

CHOCOLATE CHIP COOKIES _____

_____

CHEESE _____

_____

CHOCOLATE _____

_____

SODA POP _____

_____

PERFUME _____

_____

GRAPE JELLY _____

_____

KITCHENS
I HAVE KNOWN AND
HALF-DESTROYED

Mom says women love a guy who knows his way around the kitchen, but I've got another theory. A woman will love any guy who doesn't immediately *destroy* her kitchen. It's easy to do a ton of damage in there!

I think I'd better just stay out of the kitchen altogether.

GEORGIA

TAKING OUT THE GARBAGE IS RAFE'S JOB (FOR GOOD REASONS!)

Mom, feel free to try to get Rafe to cook. If his meat loaf ends up being more like charcoal briquette loaf...

...at least I can eat toast with cinnamon. But please stop trying to teach him how to do laundry! My favorite white top is now splotchy pink, and my favorite pink top is now blobby brown! Either ban Rafe from the laundry room or raise my allowance so I can buy new tops every time Rafe ruins them.

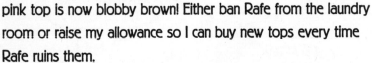

Sorry, Georgia.

No problem! See you when I get back from the mall with my new top.

Brilliant idea! I take that back— Rafe, do all the laundry you want!

AM I THE ONLY KID WHO HATES POPCORN?

I know this won't be a very popular opinion. But popcorn is a horrible snack, for so many reasons. First off, the kernels get stuck in your teeth. Always. No matter how careful you are, an hour later you have to floss your teeth like crazy to get them out. Even then, a week—maybe even a year—later, you'll find a kernel still hanging around. With all those seeds in my mouth, I'm surprised my tongue hasn't turned into a rolling cornfield.

I hate this stuff!

And no matter how much butter you ask the clerk at the movie theater to put on top, by the time you eat your way to the bottom, you're eating butter-free popcorn. Plus those tough little popcorn pebbles can break one of your teeth wide open. Crummy popcorn has ruined the endings of so many movies for me. Every time I see the end of *Harry Potter,* all I can think about is horrible popcorn. Making popcorn at home is no better. You'll never get ALL the corn to pop.

So...why can't I stop eating it?!

CHECK IT OUT, MOM: APPLE PIE IS THE BEST

Everybody in my town knows my mom makes the best apple pie anywhere. So why does she bother making other kinds of pie?

Every time I see a cherry, blueberry, or pumpkin pie on the counter, I wish I could go back in time and say, "Hey, Mom, I appreciate that you're baking a pie, but why not make it an apple pie? There are some apples right over there in the fruit bowl. This isn't difficult."

Whenever I bring it up, Mom rolls her eyes, but I don't see what the big deal is. If an apple pie is as easy to make as other types of pie, why not make an apple pie every time? I don't get it! And don't even get me started on lemon bars.

MY TURN (NOT FOR MOM'S EYES): PUDDING CUPS REIGN SUPREME

I like any kind of baked good Mom makes, but I have to say, I'm always disappointed when she makes pudding from scratch. I appreciate that she puts a lot of effort into it, but...here's the thing: I *love* ready-made pudding cups so much.

We're not talking "yeah, I really like them." We're talking "if I don't eat at least one a day I will self-combust!" I don't know what's in them. Pixie dust? Leprechaun gold? Debris from a shooting star?

Okay, that's pretty unlikely. But it's some kind of magical substance that makes packaged pudding cups totally addictive. And if eating them constantly is wrong, I don't want to be right.

For once.

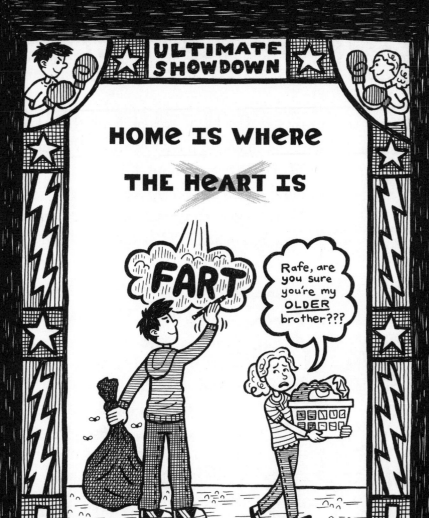

THE PROBLEM WITH MAKING YOUR BED

You'd think any kid who hates school as much as I do would be happy to spend plenty of time at home, right? WRONG. There are so many annoying things about being at home. Pretty sad, isn't it?

For example: Who was the *genius* who decided we should all make our beds? That has to be the

Why, why, WHY? This is a question in the minds of millions of Kids, not to mention hotel cleaning staff across the country.

Should we tell him why, why, why?

Nah! Let him "sleep tight" and then WE will bite!

dumbest chore ever invented. And how did it get passed down from generation to generation?

I don't know why I should have to make my sheets and blankets all nice and neat when I'm just going to mess them up half a day later.

The things we do for an allowance.

THE DUMBEST CHORES
OF ALL TIME

Make a list of the top ten dumbest chores you've ever done:

10. _____

9. _____

8. _____

7. _____

6. _____

5. _____

4. _____

3. _____

2. _____

And the #1 dumbest chore of all time is....

1. _____

Here are some chores I hate. Georgia? She loves chores, so this would be her "Favorite Things to Do on the Weekend" list.

Making the bed
Mowing the lawn
Taking out the trash
Piling the recycling
Picking up pet poop
Scrubbing toilets
Washing dishes
Pulling weeds
Clearing the table
Setting the table

Cleaning up bedroom
Vacuuming
Spelling *vacuum* (what's up with all those *u*'s?)
Walking the dog
Putting toys away
Feeding the pets
Doing laundry
Washing the car
Raking leaves

How can she actually ENJOY doing that?

Hmm mmm

VACATIONS ON THE MOON

Who needs a vacation? I sure do. Between all those chores, school, and putting up with Georgia, I'm really wiped out these days.

The trouble is, Mom never takes my vacation suggestions seriously! This year, when she asked where we wanted to go, I said the moon. Hear me out before you call me crazy: There are a lot of companies selling vacation packages to the moon! And as an artist, it would be good for me to see new landscapes I can draw.

When Mom asks where we want to go on vacation,

what she really means is, do we want to go camping in the woods or do we want to go camping even farther into the woods?

NAME YOUR VERY OWN DREAM VACATION

Here's a shortcut to describing your ultimate vacation. Use this format and fill in the blanks:

THE __(A)__ , __(B)__ -ING, AND __(C)__ VACATION

(A) If you could go anywhere on vacation, what kind of place would you go? _____

_____

(B) If you could do anything on vacation, what would you do? _____

_____

(C) If you could eat anything on vacation, what would you eat? _____

_____

Mine would be: The <u>BEACH</u>, <u>JET SKI</u>-ING , and <u>WAFFLE FRIES</u> vacation.

WRITE YOUR ULTIMATE VACATION HERE:

THE _____ , _____-ING,
　　　　　(A)　　　　　　　　　(B)

AND _____ VACATION
　　　　　(C)

ROAD TRIPS MUST BE AVOIDED AT ALL COSTS!

I was pretty excited when my mom said she was going to take us somewhere different on vacation this summer. Maybe we were finally going someplace *cool*!

I was ready to get out of town, chow down at good restaurants like BK and Taco Bell and Applebee's every night, and see some cool stuff. What Mom didn't tell us was that it was going to be a *road trip* vacation. *Ugh.* Is there anything worse than sitting in the car with your mom and your grandma and your sister for ten hours...*each way*?! Staring out the window for hours on end, passing signs that say WELCOME TO WHEREVER and YOU ARE NOW LEAVING WHEREVER, listening to your mom sing her favorite song, like, ten times in a row. It may sound like a vacation, but it's really detention on wheels.

MIDDLE SCHOOL BINGO

If you're stuck in a car with your sibs trying not to kill each other and you need some backseat boredom busters, never fear! You can be the very first to try out an amazing new game I like to call Middle School Bingo!

INSTRUCTIONS:

Cut out the Rafe faces. Put double-sided sticky tape on the back of each. Ta-da! You've made your own Middle School Bingo stickers! Now, to play the game, get some friends together and place your stickers on any scorecard item that you see in your school. (And remember where you saw it, because your friends may demand proof!) The first player to get five in a row—horizontally, vertically, or diagonally—is the winner.

Feel free to draw on Rafe's face. He ate pizza, French fries, AND chocolate yesterday. Pimples should be popping up all over.

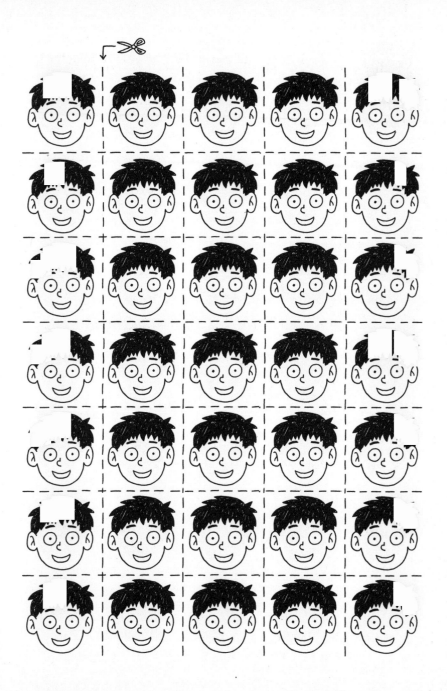

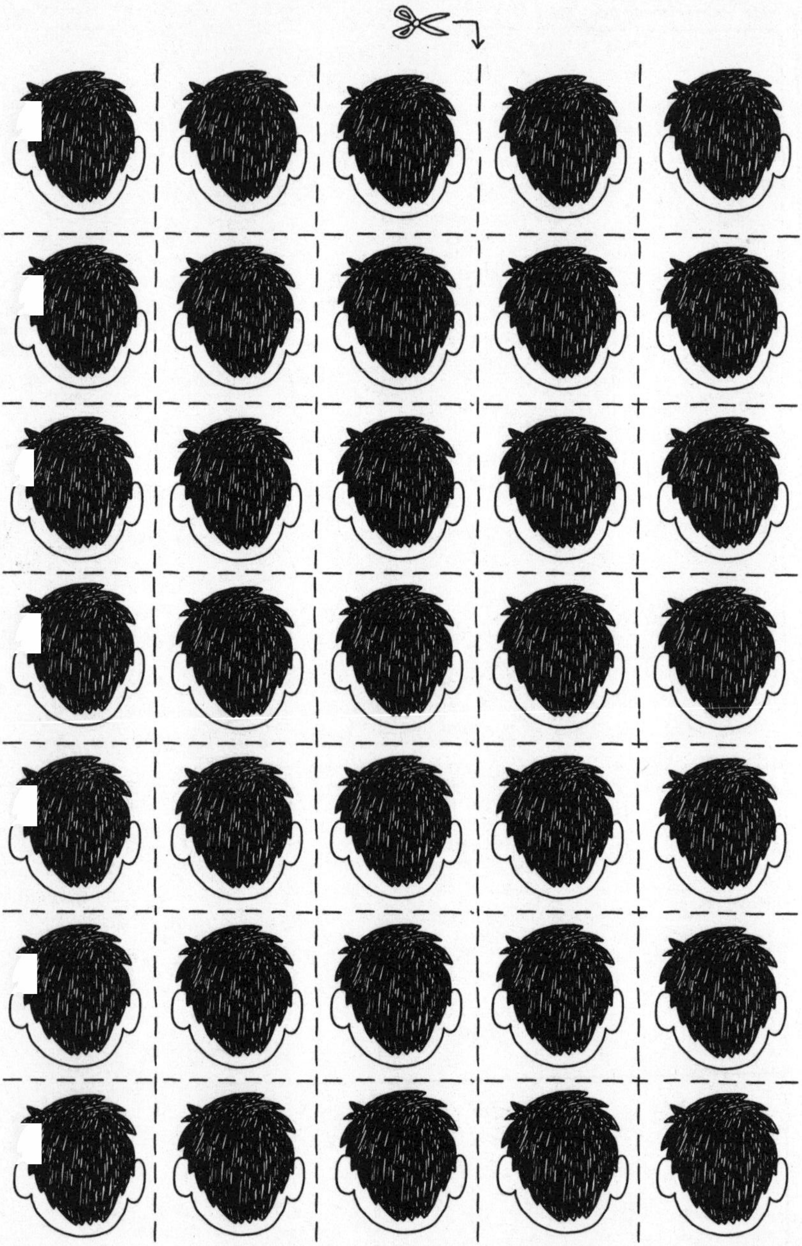

R A F E - O

WATER FOUNTAIN	BLUE DRY-ERASE MARKER	SCHOOL BUS	STAPLER	RED PEN
ANNOYING BOY BAND POSTER	CAFETERIA WORKER	APPLE	TROMBONE	LIBRARY BOOK
ANTI-BULLYING POSTER	DIGITAL CLOCK	FREE SPACE	PICTURE OF A DOG	YELLOW LUNCH BOX
PAIR OF CROCS	AMERICAN FLAG	PINK BACKPACK	*I FUNNY* BOOK	GRAPH PAPER
PHOTO OF OLD DUDE FROM HISTORY	WALL MAP	EQUATION	PROTRACTOR	JUICE BOX

ROADSIDE ATTRACTIONS ACTUALLY WORTH SEEING!

WHERE ON EARTH* WILL YOU FIND THESE AWESOME ATTRACTIONS?

*Hint: They're all in the United States. Choose from the list below!

ROSWELL, NEW MEXICO _____

BIRMINGHAM, ALABAMA _____

GRANGER, WASHINGTON _____

CHESTER, ILLINOIS _____

OCHOPEE, FLORIDA _____

BLUE EARTH, MINNESOTA _____

A. VULCAN THE IRON MAN

B. STATUE OF POPEYE

C. LARGEST JOLLY GREEN GIANT
   STATUE

D. SKUNK APE RESEARCH
   HEADQUARTERS

E. INTERNATIONAL
   UFO MUSEUM

F. DINOSAUR TOWN
   WITH VOLCANO TOILETS

BLAME THE DOG

As you probably noticed from our disagreements up to this point, Georgia's a big tattletale who's always trying to get me in trouble. I used to get into a lot less trouble when our dog Ditka was still around, which is why I am a big fan of getting another one. Because you know what dogs are good for? *Taking blame.*

Eat a piece of food off the counter? Blame it on the dog. Get the carpet muddy? It must've been the dog. Break one of your sister's dolls? No problem, it was the dog. Let a fart rip? *Definitely* the dog.

GEORGIA

THE TRUTH ABOUT CATS

Forget dogs. Cats are the way to go if you need a distraction from something you've done wrong. Our mom can't resist them, so if she's about to yell at me for, say, not vacuuming the living room when I was supposed to, all I have to do is hold up a furry little diversion.

You can use cats to sidetrack your mom anytime you want (as long as there's a treat in it for the cats). Seriously—they're not the brightest. I've seen my cat chase its own tail. And go bonkers about a little red dot of light from a laser pointer. And try to intimidate its own reflection for hours.

You know, that reminds me of someone else I know who isn't that smart....

YOUR OPINION ABOUT PETS (OR, AS GEORGIA CALLS THEM, ANIMAL COMPANIONS)

On the next page, circle your choice in each pair of pets. Then work your way down to see what's going to follow you home. (Well, that's what you're going to tell your parents.) Then give your pet a name.

?!

Don't try this at home!

How many people have alligators in their homes?

I think you mean "Don't try this at the ZOO."

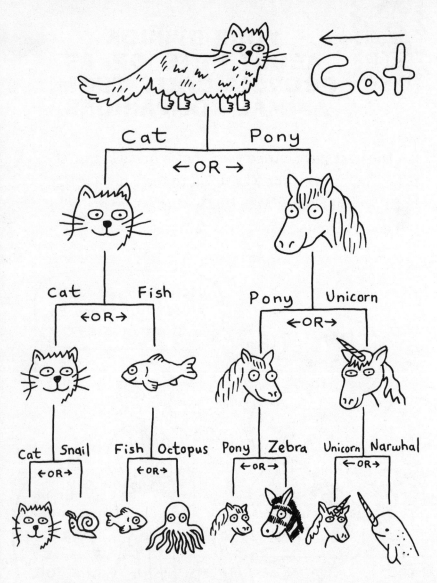

Cat

Cat OR Pony

Cat OR Fish

Pony OR Unicorn

Cat OR Snail

Fish OR Octopus

Pony OR Zebra

Unicorn OR Narwhal

YOUR NEW PET IS A(N) _____,

AND ITS NAME IS _____.

GEORGIA

ONLINE DATING IS NOT FOR MOMS!

I usually love the Internet, but right now I want to smash it into a million pieces.

SMASH!

Yes, Rafe, before you say anything, I *know* the Internet isn't an object that I can destroy by breaking our computer. I just really want to hit something!

You see, my mom signed up for an online dating site.

I know, right? Rafe and I barely see her because she has to work so much, and now she's going to spend her tiny amount of free time looking at profiles and doing her hair and makeup and meeting strangers. Last time we ordered something online it was a toaster oven that broke about five minutes after we got it out of the box. So I don't have any better expectations for the kind of boyfriend Mom could find online. I just hope he comes with a return policy.

RAPHAEL? IT'S, LiKE, THE TWENTY-FIRST CENTURY, RiGHT?

I hate to say it, but I kind of agree with Georgia on that last subject. Mom's pretty great *most* of the time, but she also had a major brain fart when she named her kids. She named me Raphael after the famous artist from... well, I don't exactly know where he's from, but he lived in practically medieval times. What's worse, I don't even get a good *nick*name for the bad full name. Everyone makes just as much fun of the name Rafe!

If she had done a little more research into that painter's personal life, maybe she wouldn't have named her only son after him. Raphael was a great artist who lived in a palace, but get this: By the time he was eleven years old, both of his parents were dead. He never got married, and for six years he was engaged to a girl he didn't even like. The only way he got out of it was when she died. And then he died himself...when he was thirty-seven. (That's younger than my mom...but don't tell her I told you that.) All I'm saying is that maybe she should have taken the naming of her child a little more seriously.

GEORGIA

MY TURN:
SO YOU WANT TO
TALK ABOUT NAMES?

Try having a name like *Georgia*. First of all, Georgia's a state, not exactly a normal name for a girl. Rafe thinks it's SUPER-funny to call me Georgia Peach, for some reason. And as soon as I make friends with someone and that person tries to give me a nickname, what happens?

Hi, Sam!

Hey, George! I mean, uh...

Don't even get me started on how much my geography teacher, Mr. Andrew Klein, loves it. And it's not just him. *Every* sub dives right in too.

Mom named me after the painter Georgia O'Keeffe, which I guess is actually cool, since her paintings are pretty. Lots of beautiful abstract flowers, plus some pretty cool cow skulls. I just wish people in school got that she's a cool person to be named after, instead of once again showing that they don't know anything they can't find on Facebook.

By the way—and I'd like your help here—what *is* my nickname supposed to be? I don't want to be George! Maybe Gigi or Gia! Any more ideas, write them down here.

_____

_____

_____

WORST NAMES EVER

Circle your (least) favorite. Then remember this page when you have kids! (By the way, these are *actual* names parents *really* gave children. In the twenty-first century. No joke.)

BOYS	GIRLS
BURGER	AMERICUS
CHOLERA	FEDORA
ESPN	GILMORE
GOODLUCK	HYSTERIA
HIPPO	PICKLE
NAVARYOUS	SESAME
POPEYE	YOGA
TRON	ZEALAND

And if your last name is Lee, make sure you name your kid Brock!

THE BEST BABYSITTING TACTIC

Speaking of babies, whoever coined the term *babysitting* had the right idea. Sometimes the only way to get the kid you're watching to stop eating glue is to literally sit on him. Too bad parents don't like it.

The thing I don't get is why these parents even have glue in their house. That kid seemed like a pretty experienced glue eater. I can't believe this was the first time it happened. The kid was a glue-eating gourmet.

THE NiGHTMARe OF BABY PHOTOS

I think you'll agree with this one. Every kid lives in fear of one thing—someone from school seeing his baby photos.

When you're born, your parents take more photos of you than they will ever take of anything else in their entire lives.

Every single one of these pictures could turn your middle school years into endless, miserable torture. Parents should never take a picture of their kids until they're in sixth grade...maybe not even then. Maybe at your wedding? Probably not. I'll bet those can be embarrassing too.

THANKS FOR THE GREAT IDEA, RAFE

Unfortunately, by the time you read this, Rafe will have already hidden his baby photos. I never knew he thought they were embarrassing. Mine are so adorable. I even have one as my Facebook profile photo. It got fifteen "likes"!

I need to find those photos of Rafe. Next time Rafe pulls a prank on me, I have to be ready to get him back. If only I had those photos, my options would be endless. I could post them online, I could photocopy them and leave them around the school, or I could mail them to Jeanne Galletta.

EXTRA! EXTRA! Rafe sucked Binky as a baby!

Gotcha! You're SO busted for plotting evil cyberbullying, Georgia!

FiND THE FACE!

Can you match the goofy
baby picture to the today picture?

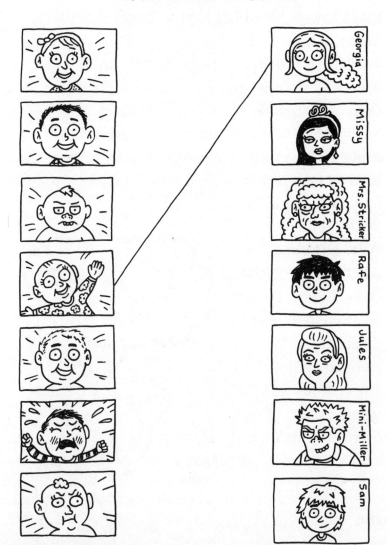

FAIRY TALES ARE FOR BIG BABIES

Speaking of babies...even when I was a little kid, I always hated fairy tales. They're totally unrealistic! I'm not talking about the spells, or the witches, or the fairies. Not even the gingerbread houses or the cranky old people who live inside them. That stuff's great. It's just that most of the heroes of these dumb stories are either really demented or really depressing. Are we supposed to pretend that any sane person would make the same lunatic decisions these weirdos make?

THE PRINCESS AND THE FROG:

Okay, I know I'm no dreamboat, but I like to think I'm way more attractive than a frog. If it's this difficult to get a girl to kiss me, there's no WAY a girl would kiss a frog, especially if she's a princess!

Lose the warts and join the football team— THEN we'll talk.

CINDERELLA: Girls *always* go for Prince Charming. What about Prince Not-So-Charming?! What about Prince Kind-of-Awkward-but-He's-a-Nice-Guy-Once-You-Get-to-Know-Him?! I want some fairy tales where the princess falls for *him*!

SLEEPING BEAUTY: Any boy who falls in love with a girl just from seeing her asleep is an idiot. He'd need to talk to her first! For all he knows, she could be obnoxious or conceited, or have a super-annoying voice, or have nothing in common with him.

THE PRINCESS AND THE PEA: If the prince is old enough to get married, what is he doing still living with his mom? He's a prince. He should be able to afford his own place! Is his kingdom bankrupt or something? If he's that poor, the princess probably isn't going to date him anyway. Then again, the girl does sleep with vegetables in her bed....

GEORGIA

MY TURN:
RAFE, WHY SO GRIMM?

Fairy tales are great! *If* you have any imagination at all—which leaves my brother out. As we've established, he's not that bright. He'd never survive in even the simplest story.

Grandma, what big teeth you have!

Seriously, dude, does your Grandma Dotty have hair all over her face and vampire teeth?

Little Rafe Riding Hood

Rafe obviously doesn't know that most fairy tales were originally written for adults. And they were about as grim and gross as *The Walking Dead* (which Rafe is not allowed to watch, but he probably finds a way to do it on his computer when Mom's at work).

So if Rafe knew anything, he'd become a world scholar of fairy tales—and he'd love it.

READY TO LiVE HAPPiLY EVER AFTER?

Create your own tale! Fill in the blanks on the following pages by choosing one of these words or phrases for each blank.

(A) fair prince; fairly normal princess; kid named Bob

(B) a magical condominium; Toronto; a suitcase

(C) incredible; awesome; amazing

(D) hairy gorilla; dragon with bad breath; flying trout

(E) cheesy nachos; birthday cake with sprinkles; Hot Pockets

(F) Scram; Begone, vile creature; I'm sorry, all operators are busy with other monsters

(G) Chillax; Whoa, dude—dial it down a notch; Y'know, I was thinking the exact same thing

(H) girls' bathroom; hall closet; garbage barrel in the school cafeteria

(I) my sister; the assistant principal; the guy who works at the drive-thru window at Burger King

(J) annoying; stupid; boring...annoying, stupid, and boring

A NOT-SO-GRIM FAIRY TALE

Once upon a time, there was a _____
(A)

who lived in _____ and had an
(B)

_____ friend named _____ .
(C)   (your name)

One day, a giant _____ hungry for
(D)

_____ came to their village and said,
(E)

" _____, where do you keep your
(A)

_____ ?" When the _____
(E)   (A)

said, "_____," _____ said
          (F)   (your name)

"_____. There's plenty of food in the
       (G)

_____. Help yourself, bro."
       (H)

   "What?" said the _____. "You
                          (A)

would help the evil _____who is really
                           (D)

_____?!"
       (I)

   "Definitely," _____ said. "Fairy tales
                      (your name)

are _____. I just want to live happily
        (J)

ever after!"

YOU CAN ILLUSTRATE A SCENE FROM YOUR AWESOME NEW TALE HERE!

You can also totally skip this page if you're sick of thinking about stupid fairy tales!

I Like Awesome Stuff; Girls Like Dumb Stuff

First, can we talk for a second about the dumb things girls say they like? Nail polish, for example.

No guy ever said, "Gee, I didn't even know that girl existed before, but now that she has pink nails, I'm going to stop reading this comic book and hang on her every word."

Hugging is definitely another one. You watch girls who barely know each other and it's like a ginormous hugapalooza when they meet in the hallway at school. Like, *every time* they meet in the hallway.

And don't get me started on malls. Girls love malls. They usually hug at the mall too—outside the nail salon. I don't get it.

I'm late for English! Stop hugging!

ERF!

MY TURN: GIRLS DON'T DO EVERYTHING FOR BOYS!

Rafe is clearly a chauvinist. (Look it up—it comes in handy around my house a lot.) Girls don't wear nail polish for boys, Rafe. We wear it to impress other girls!

Last week I wore my new midnight-blue nail polish and painted on little yellow stars. My fingertips were like a planetarium. I could practically smell Missy's jealousy.

Of course, Rafe would never understand. The most effort he puts into his appearance is making sure he's wearing pants, and even then he's not very careful.

Which is probably why no one ever wants to hug him. News flash, Rafe: Hugs are *nice*! And going to the mall with your friends (another concept you wouldn't understand) is *fun*. You're lucky you have me around to explain these things to you.

KILNS SHOULD BE BANNED EVERYWHERE

> I know, I know. I tried my best to get this stupid topic thrown out of the book. My brother is the most stubborn person on Earth!

Georgia loves throwing around words no one understands. Well, now it's my turn. Let me tell you about kilns—and why they are the worst idea anyone has ever had, ever.

A kiln is like a big oven that's supposed to bake your clay when you're doing sculpture for art class. What it actually does is take a sculpture you've spent weeks getting just right, and blow it up. Every single time I put something in a kiln, my sculpture explodes! Don't get me wrong—I love

179

explosions as much as the next kid, but only when the thing exploding isn't something I'm being graded on!

GEORGIA

MY TURN: NOBODY CARES ABOUT KILNS, RAFE!

I told Mr. Stubborn about ten thousand times: No kilns!

For starters, who cares? To put that another way—nobody cares! Except one person! And he's barely human.

I'm not even going to dignify it with a response. Instead, I'll do a totally new rant of my own, although I'll stick with the theme of art class.

You know what's great about art class? The art!

You know what's not great about art class? The class!

When I draw in my sketchbook, it's a pretty personal thing. But my teacher always makes us show at least one piece we drew at the end of the period, probably as a way to make sure everyone is actually working, but also as a way to torture me.

DRAWING
FAST AND FURIOUS

You think that's bad? Try figure drawing, which is where we take turns modeling for the class (clothes on, of course!) while everyone else draws us.

Here's the catch: You have to draw REALLY fast. We usually do a five-minute drawing, a two-minute drawing, a one-minute drawing, then a thirty-second drawing. And no, that wasn't a typo. I said *thirty seconds*. Then the teacher goes around and judges you based on what you were able to draw in *thirty seconds*.

If that isn't bad enough, sometimes you have to draw people you...you know...kind of like. And when they come over to see how you've done in *thirty seconds*, it's never going to be a great reaction.

YOUR TURN! THIRTY SECONDS...*GO!*

GEORGIA

A WARNING ABOUT RAFE'S ART SUPPLIES

Speaking of drawing stuff 24/7/365...

Rafe, you need to start being neater with your art supplies! It's not just your charcoal that gets everywhere; it's your paint. Today I found a huge, tubular blob of dried brown paint on the living room floor. You *know* what I thought it was!

Naturally, I told Mom. Hey, don't look at me like that! Rafe totally deserved to be squealed on. Mom was about to ground Rafe, until he picked up the hardened paint and proved it wasn't, well, you know. Long story short, Rafe got off scot-free and I got a lecture about being a tattletale. Does that sound fair to you?

Also, now that I think about it, why am I telling you this on one of *my* pages? Rafe sort of came off as the hero. Maybe I have the flu or something?

SQUEALER

A POP QUIZ FOR ARTIST WANNABES (AND THE REST OF YOU TOO!)

Quick! (This is another of those thirty-second drawings I warned you about!) Using this outline, draw a really cool Angry Kitten. You know, like a cute kitten—but one that's got some Angry Bird in it.

FFT! FFT!

GRR! GRR!

You probably guessed it already, but the "angry kitten" idea was all mine. Georgia just wanted to draw regular kittens....

BO-RING!

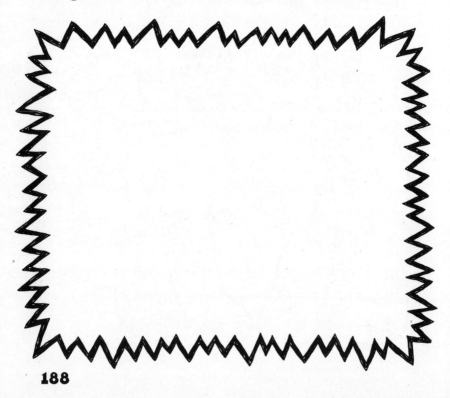

FREESTYLE DRAWING!

Time to draw anything you want. Need some inspiration? Okay, how about a soccer player who's part centipede? Or maybe a caveperson facing off with a saber-toothed tiger? It's your call. You can even do another Angry Kitten. An Angry Kitten hawking up giant hair balls that are crushing a dog's squeak toys. Whatever. Just draw the first thing that comes to mind and make it AWESOME.

GEORGIA

WE STINK (BUT OUR NAME IS AWESOME)

Let's move on to something *I'm* the expert in: music! My brother kind of forced my band into using the name We Stink for our first gig, but since then, it's actually grown on us. We discussed other options, but We Stink has just become so...us.

Besides, band names are surprisingly hard to come up with. Have you ever tried? Why don't you go for it right now? Write down the three best band names you can think of.

_____

_____

_____

Hmm, actually...those are pretty good. Mind if I steal the second one? You do? I guess we'll just stick with what we've got.

GEORGIA

GUiTARS CAN BE REALLY DANGEROUS— TRUST ME

When you see people playing guitar on TV, they don't usually wince in pain, right?

Owie! Owie! Owie!

I don't know how they do it. Playing guitar hurts so much! See, to get a good sound, the strings have to be very tightly wound, which means that when you strum them or try to hold them down, it really hurts your fingers! I'm thinking fingers covered in bandages should be my signature look. Maybe it'll become a fad once I'm a famous musician.

What bands and singers do you love?

_____

_____

_____

What bands and singers aren't you so crazy about?

_____

_____

What kind of instruments do you wish you could totally rock?

_____

_____

_____

If you're already an amazing musician, what are your favorite songs to play on your instrument?

_____

_____

_____

What songs do you wish you *never* had to play again?

_____

_____

_____

What are some songs you wish you could play perfectly?

_____

_____

_____

GEORGIA

we NeeD A HiT!

We Stink needs a hit song. And since we don't have time to learn new music, it has to be to the tune of "Row, Row, Row Your Boat," which everybody in the band already knows from, like, kindergarten. Don't worry, songwriting is easy. Just fill in a few simple blanks!

(A) ONE-SYLLABLE VERB (*WALK, GRAB, HOP*, ETC.):

_____

(B) ONE-SYLLABLE NOUN (*COW, LAMP, BRAIN*, ETC.):

_____

(C) TWO-SYLLABLE ADVERB (*BADLY, CALMLY, DAILY*, ETC.):

_____

(D) ONE-SYLLABLE NOUN THAT RHYMES WITH *CAT*:

_____

(E) THREE-SYLLABLE ADVERB (*HASTILY, ICILY, MIGHTILY*, ETC.)

_____

(F) DIFFERENT ONE-SYLLABLE NOUN THAT RHYMES WITH *CAT*:

_____

194

NOW, INSTEAD OF:

Row, row, row your boat
Gently down the stream
Merrily, merrily, merrily, merrily
Life is but a dream

DO:

_____ , _____ , _____ ,
(A)   (A)   (A)

your _____
(B)

_____ *up the* _____
(C)   (D)

_____ , _____ , _____ , _____
(E)   (E)   (E)   (E)

Life is but a _____
(F)

195

Don't worry, I'll add a few awesome guitar riffs, and I guarantee that not only will it be our next hit (okay, well, our *first* hit)—it'll totally blow the roof off our garage. That's our trademark, by the way.

I MAY BE A
TATTLETALE, BUT
RAFE IS A THIEF

This one gives me the shivers.

I have suspicions, readers, and they are not good! Rafe was listening to us yesterday at band practice, and one of my bandmates, Mari, asked him what his favorite color is. I didn't think much of it because Mari asks weird questions *all the time.*

But then—next practice—Mari had changed her hair from its usual turquoise to red...Rafe's favorite color.

Could it be possible? Could Rafe be trying to steal my friend? Could Mari be trying to impress *my brother*?! Could she (or anyone) have a crush on Rafe? This is too repulsive for me to even talk about!

MY TURN:
CAN'T A GUY JUST
LiKE A COLOR?

Red is the color of my favorite football team,
the Wisconsin Badgers. It's the color of apples,
which go in apple pie. It's half of the colors you
see in the McDonald's logo. And, you know, the
American flag has some red in it.

All I'm saying is, I liked red before Georgia's
friend (whatever
her name is)
changed
her hair.

Not that
I care or
anything.
Not that I
really even
noticed
when she
did it! But
red hair is
pretty cool,
I guess.

Hi, Rafe!

Oh, uh . . .
hey, Mari.

INSECT INVADERS OF DOOM

Girls are SO annoying, right? Worse than mosquitoes. Even worse than *bees*, which rank as number one on my list of most annoying insects. They seem to follow me everywhere.

I don't get it. We can put a man on the moon. We can travel faster than the speed of sound. We can make Doritos that taste like buffalo wings *and* ranch dressing at the same time. But we can't do anything about these bees flying around everywhere, even inside your house. Even at night. Threatening to fly up your nose or in your mouth while you're sleeping.

World, we need to get our priorities straight. Scientists out there, listen up: Before you decide to go researching something else, you need to focus on making it so bees can't bite me. We've got seedless grapes, so why not stingless bees? And if you could do something to keep them from attacking me when I chuck a water balloon at their hive, that would be great too.

To <u>bee</u> continued.

RAFE, ARE YOU ACTUALLY TRYING TO DESTROY THE EARTH?

Are you the only kid in the world who doesn't know yet that we *need* bees? It's actually a huge problem in the world right now. You might think bees are chasing you around, but the fact is, bee populations are decreasing. There are so few bees that a lot of farmers have to rent them to pollinate their crops. Without

bees to help pollinate, crops don't thrive and reproduce, right?
Then we're stuck with a major food supply problem.

Wait a second....

Rafe starts getting ideas about using science to stop bees,
and now bee populations are decreasing?

This is clearly all his fault! I'm telling Mom!

THINKING GREEN IS WAY BETTER THAN SEEING RED

Rafe is all about getting angry and annoyed. I like to be part of the solution, not the problem. For example, last week I helped out the environment by planting a tree in my backyard.

It was so exciting...for about a day. You see, trees do not grow fast. At all.

I know that eventually it'll be good for the planet that I planted the tree, but it would be nice to see the results a little sooner. Is there any way we can make that happen?

Cell PHONeS: CAN'T We JUST GO BACK TO WRITING LeTTerS?

Ha! Only a tree hugger like Georgia would sit outside and try to watch one grow. You can water it and give it nutrients and even sing to it as much as you want (yes, I've seen her do this)—it won't grow any faster.

Speaking of slow, I have *the* slowest smartphone in the world. Mom won't buy me a nice one because she says I don't need it for anything more than letting her know I got home safely. And supposedly mine *looks* like the four-hundred-dollar version, so I should be happy. But people somehow always know I have a cheap phone.

Do the kids at my school have a special cheap-phone sense or

Rafe, you get a bonus point for this one. I totally agree.

something? Kind of like seeing ghosts, only more pretentious? Oh, and if you didn't know, *pretentious* means you think you're better than everyone else. That's one big word I know by heart, because it's so useful in our house (you know, the house where Georgia also lives).

THE HiDDEN DANGERS OF ROBOTS

When it comes to technology, though, there are times when less is more. For example: I would never want a robot friend.

Sure, it *sounds* cool. A robot friend could have laser eyes and superstrength. But in my experience, friends can quickly turn into enemies. If I don't get my friend a good enough birthday gift, I don't want him to destroy me.

I already have enough problems in my life. So, scientists, take your time with robots. Now, something that could give ME laser eyes, that I could use.

MY TURN:
ROBOT PARANOiA IS
TOTALLY UNCALLED FOR!

I think having a robot friend would be a lot of fun. It could help me study. Plus, I could program it to come up with witty comebacks when the Princess Patrol picks on me or my friends.

Did you get hit by a car, or is that your attempt at wearing makeup?

AT LEAST IF I GOT HIT BY A CAR, I WOULDN'T BE HERE TO SEE THOSE HORRIBLE SHOES. DUMPSTER-DIVE MUCH?

Did you get hit by a car, or is that your attempt at wearing makeup?

AT LEAST....
DUMPSTER...
DUMPSTER...
DIVE! DIVE!
DIVE!

BZZT!

BZRT!

GZZp!

Of course, if my robot friend had as many problems as my computer does, it might do more harm than good.

209

MOVIES: HOLLYWOOD JUST DOESN'T GET IT!

Okay, this has to be said: If a movie doesn't have at least one massive explosion, what's the point?

If I can persuade my mom to drive me and a friend to the movies and pay eight dollars for my

ticket, I want to see a bunch of stuff blowing up.
And maybe a high-speed car chase or three.

What I don't want to see is kissing, crying,
hugging, or puppies. Hollywood, you've been
warned. Also, let's cool it with singing movies.
Especially really long ones that moms drag the
whole family to see.

WHY NOBODY WATCHES TV ON "REGULAR TV" ANYMORE

If you can record something and skip the commercials, why wouldn't you? Because it seems like 95 percent of all ads on TV just aren't funny.

Why aren't *all* commercials funny? It just doesn't make sense! There are some commercials I'd watch without being forced to, like anything with a monkey or a dog. But not obnoxious commercials where it's just some guy yakking about a terrible accident.

Why even bother putting that junk on TV? No one's going to pay attention. Also, being funny isn't that hard. For five bucks and a chocolate bar, I'd make their commercial way better!

TV CAGE MATCH

Let's get serious here, because this is something we all have to deal with on a daily basis.

We only have one TV at my house, so when you want to watch your show, you'd better be ready for a fight. Mom is obsessed with this show where a lady cooks for half an hour. That's all she does, cook and tell you what she's doing while she cooks. If I wanted to do that, I could hang out with the lunch ladies in the cafeteria!

> I like to use two-week-old rump steak. It gives the perfect rancid flavor.

Georgia will die if she doesn't watch *Pink Pony Sunshine Flowers Glitter Time* (I don't know the actual title, but you get the point), even though it's always on at the same time as my weekly *Monster Truck Takedown* show.

So I say we let the shows fight it out themselves. If we could get all the characters in a cage together somewhere, I think we know who'd come out the winner.

COUCH POTATO CENTRAL

Okay, it's time to channel your inner couch potato and tell us your opinion about the best and worst things on TV.

TOP TEN FAVORITE SHOWS

1. _____

2. _____

3. _____

4. _____

5. _____

6. _____

7. _____

8. _____

9. _____

10. _____

TOP TEN WORST SHOWS

1. _____

2. _____

3. _____

4. _____

5. _____

6. _____

7. _____

8. _____

9. _____

10. _____

TOP TEN TV SHOWS NOBODY KNOWS YOU WATCH BUT YOU ACTUALLY LIKE (YOU HAVE TEN OF THEM?!)

Season one on DVD

1. _____

2. _____

3. _____

4. _____

5. _____

6. _____

7. _____

8. _____

9. _____

10. _____

CREATE YOUR OWN TV SHOW!

Just fill in the blanks on the next page and move to Hollywood. Use one of our words or write in your own.

(A) talkative; sleepy; fire-breathing

(B) refrigerator; kleptomaniac; race car driver

(C) perky; irritating; bored

Let's do lunch!

(D) potato; cheerleader;
    Supreme Court justice

(E) merrily; clumsily; secretly

(F) flop; dance; swim

(G) Brussels; the Atlantic Ocean; the moon

(H) feather factory; funeral parlor; jelly bean shop

TITLE:

THE _____ _____
      (A)   (B)

THE HILARIOUS NEW SITCOM!

A(N) _____ _____
       (A)   (B)

FALLS IN LOVE WITH A A(N) _____
                             (C)

_____! TOGETHER, THEY
    (D)

_____ _____TO
   (E)   (F)

_____ AND GET A JOB
    (G)

AT THE WORLD'S WACKIEST

_____.
    (H)

TUESDAYS AT EIGHT!

WAIT A MINUTE! IS RAFE TRYING TO SKIP ME? NO WAY!

I watch TV sometimes, but I try not to let things get too cheesy. I don't watch all that reality stuff. Mostly I watch television that betters the mind, like this one documentary program that

This culturally enlightening program is so fascinating.

explores the lives of three sisters in California.

What? No, I'm not talking about *Keeping Up with the Kardashians*! I'm talking about that classy documentary series called...

fine, you got me. I love *Keeping Up with the Kardashians*! But it's my *one* guilty pleasure...and *The Voice*...and *Here Comes Honey Boo Boo*.

I don't like where this conversation is going. Let's change the subject. Quick!

CHOOSE ONE!

222

SECRET CONCEPT—OR, FRIENDS SHARE

Well, this book has been fun. I think so, anyway. I actually haven't told a lot of people about the things I've told you in this book. I know it's a lot to ask you to keep my secrets for me, especially when we've never met in person.

Tell you what, how about a little give-and-take? I'm telling you my secrets, so you can tell me one of your own. On the lines below, write something you've never told anyone before. It can be silly, yucky, or embarrassing, and I promise not to tell anyone! If you don't want to, that's okay too.

_____

_____

_____

_____

_____

_____

_____

_____

FOR COURAGE SHOWN
IN WRITING DOWN
A
REALLY
BIG
SECRET

YOUR TURN TO RANT!

You've heard us rant about anything and everything that bugs us. Now it's time for you to write your own rant! It's harder than it looks, though, so I made something to show you the ropes. Fill in the blanks to complete your very own Rafe-style rant!

(A) something that ticks you off, bugs you, or just generally annoys you: _____

_____

(B) any word that means the same thing as *stupid*:

_____

(C) how you like to creatively express your anger:

_____

(D) words your mom might use to describe broccoli or homework: _____

(E) the worst homemade birthday gift you can think of: _____

(F) a disgusting bodily function: _____

(G) an item of clothing or a body part: _____

_____

(H) another word for *idiot*: _____

NOW, JUST FILL IN THE BLANKS BELOW WITH YOUR ANSWERS, AND RANT AWAY!

Ugh! _____ is so _____!
           (A)   (B)

It makes me _____ every time! My
              (C)

mom tells me it's _____, but she also
                 (D)

likes _____, so her opinions are clearly
     (E)

wrong. If I have to see one more _____,
                           (A)

I seriously think I'm going to _____ all
                       (F)

over my _____! And you know
       (G)

who's to blame? The _____
                 (H)

who created _____!
       (A)

NOW THAT YOU'RE A PRO, IT'S TIME TO RANT SOLO. READY. SET. RANT!

_____

_____

_____

_____

_____

_____

_____

_____

_____

_____

_____

_____

_____

_____

_____

ALMOST DONE

Well, that just about finishes our book and the contest between me and Rafe — and I think it's pretty obvious that I'm the winner (over Rafe, I mean, not over you).

From bullying to bacon — well, I'll just let the work speak for itself. That's called sportsmanship. No, make that sports **GIRL** ship.

No way! I was funnier than Georgia. Who do you think did the Fart Chart, not to mention the genius burp diagnosis?

Oh yeah, and let's not forget the Bizarro-Rant. Even Georgia said it was decent. I rest my case. Coming from Georgia, that's like an A-plus!

AND DONE

"It's not *just* about being funny, you know! I had a lot of important stuff to say—like teaching you about how important bees are."

"I did too. Like, uh, um, you know what I'm trying to say—"

"Like how to tell what kind of fart you had? Or what kind of burp? C'mon, Rafe, book a return trip to Planet Earth."

"Okay, I'm back on Earth. How about you? Like anyone cares about your stupid band and the teensy little cuts you get playing your guitar all wrong."

"Your taste in music is like your taste in sneakers. Smelly!"

"Then why's your band called We Stink?"

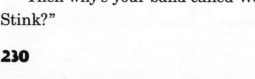

"It's ironic!"

"Your *face* is ironic."

"That doesn't even make sense! And neither did that rant about the Gettysburg Address."

"You know what—you *are* a Goody Two-Shoes. You know that, right?"

"Stop it!"

"Make me stop. Go all Library Rage on me. No, wait! Don't. Okay, okay, enough. Truce!"

"I guess...truce. One more thing, though. Do our readers know that you and I are just kidding? Just expressing our opinions. But when the chips are down, you always have my back."

"Yeah, reader, *mostly*, we're kidding. Of course, one of us might have better opinions than the other. But we definitely have each other's backs. So don't you ever say anything bad about my *sister*."

"And don't say anything really bad about my brother! Leave that to me."

"You always have to get the last word, don't you?"

"Yep. And I can keep this up until we're both old and wrinkled. Go ahead and try me. Go for it. Don't be afraid. What are you waiting for?"

MANY YEARS LATER

"Stop mumbling to yourself. You're still ridiculous."

"You're still a Goody Two-Shoes. Hey, I just came up with a name for your church choir group: We're Old but We Still Stink."

"Well, even though it's all wrinkly, I've still got your back."

"Ditto. Watch your step there, Georgia Peach."

"Don't get your cane caught in the drain."

"Is your mouth getting a little tired from so much flapping?"

"Nope. Yours?"

FART!

"I absolutely refuse to end this book like that. I refuse. I won't do it. Say something else."

BURP!

"I can live with that. I guess I have to!"

"Yup. We're stuck with each other for a few more years!"

If you liked hanging with the Khatchadorians, check out these other hilarious adventures by James Patterson!

THERE'S SOMETHING FOR EVERY READER!

HIGH ADVENTURE ON THE HIGH SEAS!

Turn the page for a sneak peek at
James Patterson's adventure series.

AVAILABLE NOW!

1

L et me tell you about the last time I saw my dad.

We were up on deck, rigging our ship to ride out what looked like a perfect storm.

Well, it was perfect if you were the storm. Not so much if you were the people being tossed around the deck like wet gym socks in a washing machine.

We had just finished taking down and tying off the sails so we could run on bare poles.

"Lash off the wheel!" my dad barked to my big brother, Tailspin Tommy. "Steer her leeward and lock it down!"

"On it!"

Tommy yanked the wheel hard and pointed our bow downwind. He looped a bungee cord through the wheel's wooden spokes to keep us headed in that direction.

"Now get below, boys. Batten down the hatches. Help your sisters man the pumps."

Tommy grabbed hold of whatever he could to steady himself and made his way down into the deckhouse cabin.

Just then, a monster wave lurched over the starboard side of the ship and swept me off my feet. I slid across the slick deck like a hockey puck on ice. I might've gone overboard if my dad hadn't reached down and grabbed me a half second before I became shark bait.

"Time to head downstairs, Bick!" my dad shouted in the raging storm as rain slashed across his face.

"No!" I shouted back. "I want to stay up here and help you."

"You can help me more by staying alive and not

letting *The Lost* go under. Now hurry! Get below."

"B-b-but—"

"Go!"

He gave me a gentle shove to propel me up the tilting deck. When I reached the deckhouse, I grabbed onto a handhold and swung myself around and through the door. Tommy had already headed down to the engine room to help with the bilge pumps.

Suddenly, a giant sledgehammer of salt water slammed into our starboard side and sent the ship tipping wildly to the left. I heard wood creaking. We tilted over so far I fell against the wall while our port side slapped the churning sea.

We were going to capsize. I could tell.

But *The Lost* righted itself instead, the ship tossing and bucking like a very angry beached whale.

I found the floor and shoved the deckhouse hatch shut. I had to press my body up against it. Waves kept pounding against the door. The water definitely wanted me to let it in.

That wasn't going to happen. Not on my watch.

I cranked the door's latch to bolt it tight.

I would, of course, reopen the door the instant my dad finished doing whatever else needed to be done up on deck and made his way aft to the cabin. But, for now, I had to stop *The Lost* from taking on any more water.

If that was even possible.

The sea kept churning. *The Lost* kept lurching. The storm kept sloshing seawater through every crack and crevice it could find.

Me? I started panicking. Because I had a sinking feeling (as in "We're gonna sink!") that this could be the end.

I was about to be drowned at sea.

Is twelve years old too young to die?

Apparently, the Caribbean Sea didn't think so.

I FUNNY
A MIDDLE SCHOOL STORY

JAMES PATTERSON
AUTHOR OF *MIDDLE SCHOOL, THE WORST YEARS OF MY LIFE*
AND CHRIS GRABENSTEIN

HA

HA

HA

HA

HA

HA

HA

an amazing (and pretty funny) **adventure!**

IN THIS STORY YOU WILL FIND...

jokes about penguins, bullies, zombies, Darth Vader, chicken nuggets, invisibility, American history, Vulcans, nachos, and way too many other awesome things to fit on this page...

INCLUDING the true story of why I, Jamie Grimm, the new kid in town, keep my past a deep secret from all my new friends. Because NOTHING will stop me on my mission to become **THE PLANET'S FUNNIEST KID COMIC!**

NO adults allowed!!
******

Laffs →

NO LAME Justin Bieber Jokes!

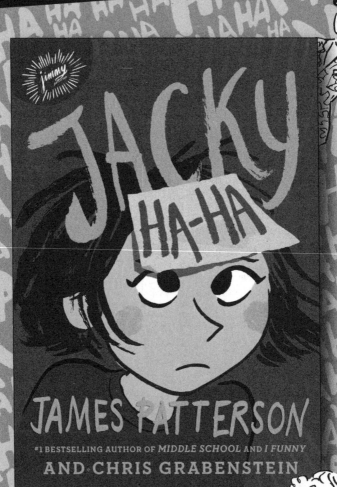

JACKY
HA-HA

JAMES PATTERSON

#1 BESTELLING AUTHOR OF *MIDDLE SCHOOL* AND *I FUNNY*

AND CHRIS GRABENSTEIN

JAMES PATTERSON received the Literarian Award for Outstanding Service to the American Literary Community at the 2015 National Book Awards. He holds the Guinness World Record for the most #1 *New York Times* bestsellers, including *Middle School, Jacky Ha-Ha,* and *I Funny,* and his books have sold more than 350 million copies worldwide. A tireless champion of the power of books and reading, Patterson created a children's book imprint, JIMMY Patterson, whose mission is simple: "We want every kid who finishes a JIMMY Book to say, 'PLEASE GIVE ME ANOTHER BOOK.'" He has donated more than one million books to students and soldiers and funds over four hundred Teacher Education Scholarships at twenty-four colleges and universities. He has also donated millions to independent bookstores and school libraries. Patterson invests proceeds from the sales of JIMMY Patterson Books in pro-reading initiatives.

JULIA BERGEN was born in New Orleans, grew up in Massachusetts, and currently lives in New Jersey with her husband.

ALEC LONGSTRETH is a cartoonist who also works as a freelance illustrator and a comics educator. Since 2002, he has been self-publishing the Ignatz Award–winning minicomic series *Phase 7*. He lives in Alameda, California, with his wife, Claire.